WHEN ANGELS BLEED

A NOVEL

JOHN ASHLEY

The characters and events portrayed in this book are fictitious. Any similarity to real persons, living or dead, is coincidental and not intended by the author.

For more information on this book and John Ashley's other works, please visit johnashleyauthor.com.

Cover Art and Design: Christian Storm

AUTHOR'S NOTE:

A WORD OF WARNING

I don't normally put trigger warnings in my books, because I think everyone expects a little violence and dark themes when they pick up a horror novel, and I don't like giving away spoilers. However, some books necessitate them more than others, and *When Angels Bleed* is by far the darkest and most graphic thing I've written so far. It is perhaps the most meaningful thing I've written as well, and there is light within these depths, friends. But be warned that the depths are dark and deep.

If you'd like to go into the book blind, you can stop reading here and skip to the first chapter. If you want to see specific trigger warnings before you proceed, you can find them on the next page.

With much thanks,

John Ashley

TRIGGER WARNINGS:

- Extreme violence and gore throughout
- Graphic depictions of a school shooting
- Graphic depictions of chattel slavery
- Graphic depictions of ancient infant sacrifice rituals
- References to/themes of sexual assault (no graphic depictions)
- References to/themes of child molestation (no graphic depictions)

"Forget not to show love unto strangers: for thereby some have entertained angels unaware."

— Hebrews 13:2

WHEN ANGELS BLEED

CHAPTER ONE

Guilt is a pain all people feel differently. Some, no matter how severe their transgressions, hardly feel its pangs at all.

At the moment, all Jason Baker felt was the ache in his legs and the stickiness between his pits and thighs. He adjusted the brim of his Iowa Hawkeyes baseball cap and cursed the 3 p.m. sun. It wasn't supposed to get this hot so far north. At least he hadn't expected it to. Scorching summers were one of many miseries he thought he'd left behind in Alabama. But misery seemed to have a nose like a bloodhound; it always found him wherever he ran.

The heat made the hope of a passing vehicle that much more inviting. So far, he'd only seen two cars going his direction: a middle-aged woman in a Chevy and a young family in a Subaru. Only the children in the back of the Subaru had even bothered looking his way. He might as well have taken the grimy thumb he'd stretched toward the road and stuck it up his ass for all the good it did. Not that Jason was surprised. No one picked up hitchhikers anymore.

He'd been walking since sunup, putting twenty-three miles between himself and Winthrop, the small town along US 20 he'd stayed the night in yesterday. After his close call there, it didn't feel nearly far enough.

"You look familiar," the man outside the bar had said, so drunk his eyes were like glossy peppermints. "I've seen your picture somewhere, man."

Jason had brushed him off, but he didn't brush off the danger. He'd dozed restlessly for a few hours on a park bench to sleep off his own stupor, then had started along Highway 20 at first light. He'd passed through Independence several hours ago but hadn't stopped. Now, Manchester was just a few miles ahead, and he'd have no choice but to stop there. He was down to the last splash of water in his canteen, and the tendons in his feet were starting to scream.

It wouldn't be wise to stay there long either, though. No one questioned the occasional drifter, even in small towns like Manchester and Winthrop. But drifters who outstayed their welcome were a different story.

Bigger cities were no good either. Sure, he could blend in a lot easier in a place like Des Moines or Sioux City, but more people meant more opportunities for someone to recognize him. As far as he was aware, news of the manhunt for him hadn't made the national media...

Not yet. Just wait until they find the rest.

...but that didn't mean much these days. With the internet, even news of a fly farting in Alabama could potentially make its way to Iowa or wherever else he decided to run.

What he needed was total isolation. Some place completely cut off from the rest of the world. The idea of solitude, even the idea of never laying eyes on another human being again, didn't bother Jason one bit. He had never needed companionship, always found it insufferable, sooner or later.

Like it or not, though, he did still need civilization.

He had tried staying in the woods for a while. It was the only way he'd managed to evade capture in the beginning when the manhunt was at its most intense and he was still trapped in the heart of the hornet's nest. However, Jason was no survivalist. Once the food he'd crammed into his backpack was gone, going back to where there were dumpsters to rummage and convenience stores to shoplift had been his only way to keep from starving.

Neither the woods nor bouncing from one town to the next was jack shit as far as long-term plans went. It made his gut roil to think about it, so he didn't. Jason Baker had lived his adult life as a predator until he made one terrible mistake. Now, he was forced to embrace the mentality of prey. Staying alive and avoiding capture for another day was all that mattered—avoiding capture most of all. Jason could live with being prey on the run, but not livestock in a cage. He'd open his neck with the Bowie knife in his pack before he let that happen. Give it one last taste of arterial blood.

Up ahead, the highway stretched on like an asphalt anaconda. He could smell the crude oil tar baking underneath the sun. It had been 93 degrees in Winthrop yesterday according to the sign outside the pharmacy—the hottest it had been all year, some old-timer had said. Maybe it was just the heat rising from the blacktop, but today felt even hotter.

He could see a green sign in the distance with the words "Manchester: 3 miles" written in white font. At least his eyes were sharp as ever. His hearing, too. Sharp as a knife fresh off the whetstone. By his own estimation, he'd been born a gifted individual.

He was calculating the time it would take to walk those last three miles when he spotted something else, just beyond the mile marker sign.

It was a dirt road that connected to the highway on the right-hand side, disappearing into the green stalks of a cornfield. Above the leaves and corn-filled husks, a trail of smoke rose up into the blue. Jason couldn't see where it was coming from, but it couldn't have been a chimney. Not in this heat.

Without even meaning to—and despite the ache in his legs—he picked up his pace. He scanned for a sign marking the dusty road but couldn't find one. That most likely meant a private road. Someone's driveway, although he didn't see a mailbox either.

Drawing closer, he rubbed his eyes with grimy fingers, unsure the whole thing wasn't some kind of heat-induced mirage. Not that a dirt road on the side of a highway was anything so spectacular as a desert oasis or a palace in the clouds. Yet the way he felt as he approached it—the bees buzzing in his stomach, the quickening of his heart—was as fantastical as any dream or nightmare he'd ever had. There was no way to explain it, but suddenly it felt as though that road had been there waiting for him his whole life.

A rusted pickup driven by a giant of a man in stained overalls passed by. Probably just the type of person, if any such person still existed, likely to offer a rugged-looking hitchhiker a ride. But Jason ignored the vehicle. He had almost reached the dirt road's wide apron where it met the highway. Once he was there, he'd be able to look down the thin path it cut through the cornfield. Able to see what wonders lay at its end.

The buzzing in his stomach spread up through his body and into his head. Tears began to pool in his eyes, tracing lines through the dirt stuck to his face and blurring his vision. Jason hurriedly wiped them with his sleeves.

When the asphalt turned to packed dirt and gravel, he had the strange compulsion to stop and take off his shoes. He remembered fragments of a Sunday school story from days forgotten, one about some guy taking his shoes off as he approached a burning bush because he was standing on holy ground.

Jason wasn't going to burn his feet on the rocks, holy ground or not, but he couldn't resist the urge to bend down and let the dust sift through his fingers. The earth here felt electric against his skin. The sprinkle of sand sparkled like gold dust in the sunlight.

He lifted his eyes and stared down the road. There was a dwelling at its end. A modest farmhouse maybe four or five hundred paces away. Wind swayed through the lush stalks on either side of the road. The leaves seemed to whisper to him as they rustled. With no hesitation, Jason rose and started down the road.

It wasn't exactly wise to wander up on someone's home in the middle of nowhere like this. A fine way to get yourself shot is what it was, but Jason didn't care. He'd already decided he'd die for whatever there was at the end of this road.

Killing for it...well, that would be even better.

CHAPTER TWO

Hell is empty, and all the devils are here. Benjamin Parker was no literature buff, but he did attend school up through the ninth grade, and that line had stuck with him all the decades since.

Today was a particularly hot day in Hell, too. His pigs had spent the entire afternoon cooling themselves in the mud, and the goats had stayed under the shade of an oak tree. Unlike such creatures free of responsibility, Benjamin had no choice but to get out and work in the heat.

Cursed is the ground because of you, he quoted the verse from Genesis in his head. *In toil you shall eat from it all the days of your life.*

Punishment is what it was. God's wrath against man. It was the reason the droughts came and yellowed the crops. The reason why life demanded so much sweat and blood. And, most certain of all, the reason for this godforsaken farm.

Benjamin looked up at the blaring sun already past its zenith and sighed. His list of chores had been piling up for weeks. There was a rock in the pig pen that needed to be dug up, a snapped wire in the fence that needed replacing, and a pile of trash that needed burning, just to name a few. Sick of the stench of it, he'd decided to deal with the trash first.

But the flames made the day's heat even more miserable. Benjamin emptied the last barrel of garbage onto the pile and wiped the sweat from his face. It wouldn't have been nearly as bad if he could have started earlier, in the coolness of dawn. Sleep was sporadic and unpredictable for him, though; sometimes his days started at sunup, other times the middle of the afternoon.

He needed to collect the eggs next. Probably should have done that first, if he'd been thinking clearly, to keep the heat from spoiling them. If he was too late and they'd already turned foul, he'd have to go without until the next morning. Going to the market for more was not—would never be—an option.

He was halfway to the plywood coop where his hens did their laying when he saw a man walking down the road.

"God almighty," he hissed through gritted teeth. "Not again."

He thought of the .30-06 inside the house, propped up in the corner near the fireplace. He thought about retrieving it and dropping the man in his tracks. For all the good it would do.

"You stupid son of a bitch," he said, turning away at last from the house and the gun inside and starting down the road with his fists clenched at his sides. "You miserable bastard. You have no idea what you've done."

The stupid son of a bitch in question was starting to come into view. He was a tall and bulky son of a bitch, too. In Benjamin's experience, the stupidest ones usually were. You don't have to be clever when you're big enough to intimidate and bully.

He looked like he hadn't showered in weeks. Mud and stains covered his clothing. A layer of dirt covered his skin and made it look darker than it probably was. Benjamin was disgusted by the sight of him, though it's not like he could have hoped for much better. This place never attracted society's finest.

When he drew close enough to see the man's face clearly, Benjamin saw exactly what he expected to. He wore the same expression they all did: that look of dazed wonder, all slack-mouthed and glossy-eyed like they just shot up heroin for the first time. Like a moth—and just as senseless as one, too—right before it burns its wings.

"What is this place?" the man asked, stopping in front of Benjamin.

"Hell, what do you think it is? It's a farm, dipshit. *My* farm."

"I wouldn't talk that way to me if I were you, old man," he said. But his words were still slow and wistful. His eyes wide and scanning every direction.

"Son, I ain't scared of you. There ain't a thing you could do to me that's not been done worse a hundred times before."

The man didn't seem to catch that last part. He didn't question it, at least. He looked too stupefied to question much of anything. "Tell me what this place is, and I'll be on my way."

Benjamin laughed at him. "Sure you will. Just turn right around and walk back the same way you came, right? Ought to be the simplest thing in the world." He was speaking in riddles now as far as the man was concerned, but Benjamin didn't care. Slow or not, the young fool would understand soon enough. "What's your name, anyway?"

"Mike."

"You got a last name?"

"Davis."

He sounded like he was lying. Benjamin had a good ear for liars. And a lot of experience with people who arrived here giving him fake names.

"Alright then, Mike Davis. You can call me Benjamin. Not Ben, and sure as hell not Benjy. Now, follow me. I got a job for you."

Mike, or whatever his name really was, followed without question. He was still under the trance that led him here, but that would wear off quickly, and it'd be a real shitshow when it did. Might as well get some free labor out of him until then, Benjamin figured. "There's a rock I need to get out of the ground. Or a boulder, more like. You know your way around a shovel?"

"A shovel?"

"That's right. Surely you've heard of it." Benjamin spat and shook his head. He wanted to grab the man by the throat and shake him out of the dream. Slap him around a bit until he opened his eyes. He'd have done that and more if he thought it would do a bit of good. But what was the point? Some things just have to be seen to be believed. And he'd see it all soon enough.

"Start digging around the edges," Benjamin said once they were inside the pig pen. A couple of sows lifted their heads to watch the two of them with inky eyes, then lowered their chins back down into the mud. "You start on the left side, and I'll start on the right. Might have to get the mule to pull her out of there once she's loosened up, but she's coming out one way or another.

And before sunset, too, so you'd better put your back into it. You don't want to be out here after dark, son."

The man stared at the shovel in his hands like it was some kind of alien artifact. "If I help you, does that mean I get to stay here?"

"Help me or not, you're stuck here either way. But if you want to sleep under my roof and share my supper tonight, then you'd better get to digging." Benjamin thought he saw the first pinprick of doubt touch the man's features then.

For the next two hours, they dug. First through the layer of mud and pig waste at the top, then through the dry, rocky soil beneath. The boulder was even bigger than Benjamin expected it to be, but that was no surprise. The worst coming to pass was never a surprise to him anymore.

By the time they'd dug enough away to wrap a rope around it, the sun was already starting to cool. Benjamin watched the man from the corner of his eye while he fastened the other end of the rope to the mule's harness. He'd been watching him the entire afternoon, witnessing the disillusion in his eyes melt more and more with each passing minute. He took pleasure in it, but it made him jealous, too. These first few hours here would be the last pleasant moments of the man's life. It had been nearly forty years since Benjamin had experienced a single pleasant moment.

It took another half hour for the mule to pull the rock from the ground and drag it through the gate into the empty pasture behind the pen. By then, the man looked like he was having a heatstroke—his skin was flushed and his legs unsteady. But the sun was no longer blazing anymore, and Benjamin knew it wasn't the heat that had put him in this state.

"I'm going to leave now," the man said. It was the first words he'd spoken since the digging started. The waver in his voice made it sound like even he knew it wasn't true.

"Knock yourself out, son," Benjamin said, gesturing toward the road.

The man dropped his shovel into the hole and started walking.

CHAPTER THREE

Jason, who loved pills and liquor like a babe loves milk, considered most highs well worth the hangover. But coming here was a high that never delivered. It had been all come up and no climax. And now the comedown was hitting like a sledgehammer.

His nerves were on fire. The knot in his chest made each breath sharp and shallow. He'd never had a panic attack before, barely even knew what the term meant. But he was pretty sure he was having one now.

He wanted to get away from this place much faster than his exhausted legs were capable of. Hard to believe, in cold hindsight, that he'd spent the entire day busting his back to help some crotchety old farmer. Even harder to believe that this place had once been so alluring when now it repulsed him to his bones.

He stumbled back down the road toward the highway, nearly tripping twice, his balance was so off. It seemed darker than it should be—like twilight already even though the sun still peeked above the top of the cornstalks to his left. The stalks cast shadows across the road that swayed with the breeze. They groaned and shuddered against the strain, their inviting, song-like whispers long gone.

The highway should have been just ahead. Maybe fifty more yards or so based on how far he'd walked. The problem was he couldn't see it. He'd had no issue seeing the house from the highway earlier. Now, the house was well behind him, yet the dirt road still stretched on with no end in sight. The cornfield looked like a green ocean disappearing into the horizon.

What is happening? What the hell *is happening?* The question repeated over and over as he continued down the endless road. He thought that maybe the old farmer had drugged him. He wanted it to be true, in a way, because at least that made sense and was a problem that time (and one dead old farmer) could make right.

Except the only opportunity the old man would've had was the one time they stopped for a water break, and they'd both drank from the same pail, pulled straight from the farmer's well. Not to mention that this entire surreal experience had begun the moment he spotted the road. Well before he and the old man ever crossed paths.

Another fifteen minutes down a road that had taken less than five minutes to walk the first time and, as much as the idea turned his stomach, he decided to turn around. If anyone knew what was happening here, it was that old man with all his reckless jabs and stupid riddles. This time, Jason would get some sense out of him, one way or another; he'd found people were willing to say and do almost anything—spill their secrets, spread their legs, betray their gods—once his blade touched their flesh.

But before he turned back, something up ahead caught his eye. It was standing in the cornfield to the right, just a few steps from the road. Stalks and leaves shrouded it, but Jason saw what looked like clothing and limbs, then a head leering over the top of the stalks, probably seven or eight feet in the air. His heart leaped in his chest. He retrieved the Bowie knife from the pocket in his backpack in one fluid motion. But by the time his fingers wrapped around the polished handle, he realized the figure was no threat.

A scarecrow is what it was. The tufts of straw jutting out from its head were the first giveaway. Relaxing a little, Jason stepped closer.

Even at 6'4 himself, he had to crane his neck to see the scarecrow's face. It was made from a burlap sack stuffed thick with straw and cinched to the pole with a stretch of old rope that looked like a noose around its neck. The burlap was stained and molded. The eyes and mouth were cut from it haphazardly, three uneven gashes forming a triangle on its face. It wore a dingy baseball cap stuck to its head with safety pins so the wind wouldn't blow it away and a red plaid shirt stuffed full of dead branches, both just as soiled as its face.

Strangest of all was the pitchfork it held. It had been fastened with twine to the scraggly ends of the branches that formed the thing's right arm. Rust had turned its steel head brown, but the trio of points as long as his forearm still looked sharp.

Jason had heard of putting scarecrows in cornfields before, but he'd never heard of arming them. For some reason, looking at the thing made him feel uneasy. When a gust of wind lifted the tattered hems of its shirt and seemed for an instant to bring the scarecrow into motion, he took a quick step back.

His heel caught a rock sticking up from the ground, and his feet went out from under him. He hit the back of his head hard against the tightly packed earth. Stars erupted in his vision. The air rushed from his lungs.

Then, just as his ears began to ring, he heard a sound like steel screeching against steel, loud enough to overwhelm the ringing. Jason was no stranger to hard knocks, but he'd never experienced anything like that from a bump on the head. As he lay there on the ground, staring up at a sky that had somehow turned full-dark—with a smattering of blood-red stars and a sickly-looking moon—the whole world flipped upside down.

He felt it turn, like the earth was on a spit roast and God had just flipped the handle. He felt his organs shift as gravity's pull seemed to change direction. For an instant, it seemed like he would plummet off the planet and into the starry abyss that now felt below him rather than above.

Just then, a dark form stepped in front of him and blocked his view.

The straw inside its burlap head smoldered with flames, sending flashes of light and streams of smoke out its ragged eyes and mouth. Branches groaned and snapped as it lifted its arms and raised the pitchfork it held high into the air. Jason screamed, but it died in his throat when the triple forks sank through his bowels and pierced his diaphragm.

The impossible thing standing over him unsheathed the pitchfork from his abdomen with a sharp jerk, sending another paralyzing current of pain coursing through his nervous system. Jason fought through it and tried to rise. As his shoulders lifted from the ground, the fork came down again. The thin spikes slipped between his ribs with ease, sank through his heart and lungs and several inches into the dirt beneath his back. This time, the pain swiftly turned to darkness.

CHAPTER FOUR

Benjamin limped into the kitchen and poured a glass of water from the pitcher. He'd pulled a muscle in his back loading the big bastard into the wheelbarrow. Pushing him all the way back to the house had not been easy either given how far he'd run.

Should have left him there, Benjamin thought. But there was a reason he didn't, and it had nothing to do with sympathy. Despite how much of a chore it had been, it was easier this way.

He glanced into the living room to make sure the man was still sleeping, although he obviously was; he didn't imagine ole "Mike" would be very quiet whenever he woke up.

Benjamin had placed him in the rocking chair (that, too, a task that killed his aching back) and fastened his arms and legs to the wood with baling wire. Who knows if it would hold him or not, strong as he looked. It would depend on how much of a fit he threw, Benjamin supposed.

He took his glass of water and sat down in the armchair across from his detainee. He sighed and rubbed his wrinkled temples. He didn't know how long he'd have to wait. Could be minutes. Could be hours.

He wondered how it had done him. The *who* was pretty obvious given where Benjamin had found him, but whatever wounds The Scarecrow had inflicted were gone now. Probably had it easy, though, all things considered; unlike a lot of the others on the farm, The Scarecrow didn't tend to draw things out.

Half an hour passed before the man began to stir. He woke quickly then, in a lurch and gasping. His eyes shot open and widened, then narrowed on the person sitting across from him. Benjamin knew well what would come next: blame. Shock and disbelief, too, fear aplenty, but mostly blame—with all its fervor directed at him.

"What the fuck did you do to me?"

Benjamin sighed. Sometimes it was a burden being right. "Nothing. Unless you count hauling you back here…and nearly breaking my back doing it, mind you. That I did do for you."

"You drugged me, didn't you?"

"Son, if I had drugs, you can bet I wouldn't share them with the likes of you. I ain't even had a sip of beer since longer than you been alive. There are no such comforts here."

Benjamin saw him flex against the wires binding his arms, testing their strength. "Let me go. Right now, old man," he said. "And I'll kill you quickly."

Benjamin grinned. "I'd sure like to let you. If only it was that simple."

"What are you talking about? Are you crazy or something?"

"How much do you remember?"

"Of what?"

"Of what happened before you woke up in that chair. Does a pitchfork ring any bells?"

The man stared at him for a second before realization dawned on him and the color drained from his face. He tilted his head to look at his chest...

Ah, so that's where he got you, then.

...and blinked dumbly when the holes he'd expected to see there were gone.

"What the...What the hell...how did..."

It seemed like this might continue for a while, so Benjamin snapped his fingers in front of the man's face. "Steady yourself there, son. You're gonna have to be real tough from here on out."

"Tell me what's going on."

"Alright. I will. But first, you have to be honest with me. For starters, what's your name?"

"I already told—"

"I know what you told me," Benjamin interrupted. "I know it's a lie, too." The man stared at him with a blank expression. A perfect poker face. "Listen, whatever it is you're running from, you outran it, son. It ain't ever gonna find you here, I guarantee."

The man glared at him for a while longer then said, "Jason Baker. That's my real name."

"That's good. I told you mine true the first time. Benjamin Parker."

"What happened to me out there?"

"You had a run-in with an Avenger."

The man—Jason—looked incredulous for some reason. "Like the goddamn superhero movie?"

"Huh?"

"Forget it. The hell is an Avenger?"

"Demons is what they are," Benjamin said. "There's five of 'em now. They're always around, I think. But they come out of hiding when The Flip happens."

"The Flip." Jason seemed to mull the word over like he already knew what it meant.

"You felt it, didn't you? Kind of a hard thing to miss. Feels like up is down and down is up there for a couple seconds. Like you're about to fall right off the face of the earth. And everything goes dark. Don't matter what time of day it is, neither."

"I felt it," Jason said, staring into the distance, clearly reliving the event.

"There's never any warning when it happens. I tried for years to find some kind of pattern to it, but there isn't one. It's more likely to happen at night, maybe twice as likely, I'd reckon, but dusk and dawn seem to be risky hours, too. It can happen three or four times a day for days on end, then sometimes there'll be weeks between Flips. The longest it's ever gone was forty days. But I wouldn't count on that happening again if I were you."

"Why am I not dead?" Jason glanced down at his chest again, as if to confirm that the ragged holes were in fact still not there. "I felt myself die."

"That's right. You did die. And then you were *resurrected*."

"By you?"

Benjamin snorted. "Hell no, not by me. I'd have left you dead even if I could bring you back. Would've been a mercy for both of us."

"Then who?"

Benjamin threw up his hands. "Shit, I don't have *all* the answers, son. All I know is when you die here, you take a quick nap, and then you come back. If you're wounded, which you always are, they'll heal by the time you wake up. Even the rips and tears in your clothes patch themselves up. Which is a good thing, I guess, because we're not getting any more."

"How do I leave?"

Benjamin chuckled, but there was more resignation than humor in it. "Now there's the million-dollar question. You let me know if you find the answer."

"What about through the fields? Or the woods?"

Benjamin was shaking his head before Jason had even finished. "It's the same thing as the road. Just goes on and on forever, don't matter which direction you go. I used to wander out there for weeks, in the early years. Until I got sick of starving to death. There's a lot of bad ways to go on this farm, but trust me, that's one of the worst."

"There has to be a way out."

Just one way, thought Benjamin. "There isn't. The quicker you accept that, the easier it's going to be." Jason stared at him, studying him. Benjamin couldn't tell how much of it he believed. Maybe not a word.

"So why am I tied up?" Jason asked, flexing his fingers.

"I imagined you might be a little...*excitable* when you woke."

"Do I look excitable?" His voice was as placid as lake water. Somehow, this made Benjamin distrust him even more.

Not that it mattered anyway, really. The worst this man could do to him would only be more of the same. Benjamin sighed and reached into his pocket, pulling out a pair of wire cutters as he stood. "Hold still so I don't cut you. Wounds don't heal here until you die, so if you mess yourself up, you've just got to live with it until one of them gets ahold of you again."

One by one, Benjamin clipped the baling wires wrapped tight around Jason's legs and forearms. The sound of snipping filled the silence between them as Jason watched without speaking the entire time. Once, Benjamin cut him on purpose, a small nick in the skin below his knee, just to see his reaction. But the man didn't even flinch.

When the last of the baling wire fell to the hardwood floor, Jason stood and rubbed his wrists. "Tell me one more thing, old man."

Benjamin detected the change in his tone, subtle but purposeful. Still on his hands and knees from clipping the leg restraints, he lowered his head and closed his eyes. *Aww hell.* "What's that, son?"

"Let's say I saw your head off, then I burn your body in that garbage pit you've got out there and dump the ashes down your well. You still gonna come back then?"

Benjamin looked up at him with hate in his eyes. "Only one way to find out."

For the first time, Jason cracked a smile. Then he planted his boot in Benjamin's face so hard it snapped his neck and killed him before his head hit the ground.

CHAPTER FIVE

Jason's chest heaved. Blood dripped from his knuckles. The old farmer twitched at his feet, his bony arms and legs bumping and knocking against the hardwood. Death spasms, for certain. No shot he was still alive. Jason had smashed his skull like an egg, stomping it over and over with steel-toed boots. He'd beat him with his fists for a while after that, but that had just been for indulgence.

The old man wasn't his usual type—not by a long shot—but the rush of it had been largely the same. Now, though, the rush was wearing off. And panic was starting to return. He still had no clue what was happening here, and thinking about it made his head spin.

One thing was for sure, he wasn't swallowing that crock of shit the old man had tried feeding him. The idea that he'd been drugged remained the most plausible explanation. The old man was some kind of nut. Must have spent too much time out here alone or too much time in the sun and finally cracked.

Well, if he wasn't cracked before, he sure was now.

Jason thought about scouring the place for money or valuables small enough to throw in his pack, but the urge to get away from this place was much more powerful than his greed. There was a darkness here. Something sinister. Old Benjamin hadn't been lying about that. He thought of the fire burning behind that scarecrow's eyes. The smell of smoke pouring from its mouth. Hallucinations, for sure, but something else, too. Something he couldn't explain and wanted far, *far* away from.

He had almost made it to the screen door when he heard the first pop. It sounded like the corpse behind him had just cracked its knuckles. Jason felt his blood turn to ice water. Even though he didn't want to, he slowly turned around.

Something moved within the smattered remains of the old man's face. There was another loud crack as his crooked lower jaw shifted back into place. Jason watched dumbstruck as the torn skin began to stitch itself back together. Even the pool of blood like a halo around his head drew back, flowing up the same pathways of his head and face it had followed down the first time. Pouring back into the wounds just before they closed like time running in reverse. When the last bruises had faded, the old man jerked. Then Jason watched his chest start to rise and fall again. The sound of his snores made Jason's skin crawl.

Kill him again, a desperate voice cried out. But it was weak and far away. The reality of the situation was screaming much louder, freezing him there in place near the door: Benjamin had been telling the truth.

It took forty-five minutes for the old man to wake. Jason didn't move the entire time.

"Son of a bitch," Benjamin groaned. "The hell is wrong with you?" He sprang from the ground, surprisingly spry for a man his age. At first, Jason was certain he would come after him, but the rage in his eyes soon softened a little. "Fixed my back at least. But don't mistake that for gratitude, boy."

"It's true." That was all Jason could manage.

"'Course it is! You mean the goddamn living scarecrow sticking a pitchfork in your innards wasn't enough for you? You are one dense bastard, you know it? And you listen to me real good, son: there's enough suffering here without you addin' more to the pot. You ever do something like that again, and I'll make sure your next dozen deaths are as slow as a cross-country bus ride. I have ways to make that happen."

Jason nodded slowly. "I won't do it again."

"Lord help me," Benjamin muttered. He glared at Jason for a while then shook his head and spat on the living room floor. "Now that you got that out of your system, are you ready to clean out your ears and listen?"

Jason nodded again and sat back down in the same rocker he'd been bound to. "Tell me about the Avengers." He thought of that monster in the cornfield again, this time without the assurance it was only a hallucination to buffer his dread. "Start with The Scarecrow."

Leon's Transgression

Leon Kingsley, who had accomplished nothing in his life by way of legacy or relationships, would've died with a whisper and been forgotten by the time he was buried if it weren't for what he was about to do.

He refused to go out like that. The world had dejected him like a bite from a rotten apple. Mocked him. Kicked him to the ground and spat on him when he reached out his hand for help. The least the world could do before he left it was learn his name.

He fastened the buckles on his body armor and pulled the straps tight. He checked the magazine in his Glock 19, then the one in his Colt AR-15. Both were brimming with brass cartridges. A total of forty-six angry little hornets between them, all tucked into their polymer nests, and hundreds more in the mags strapped to his vest. Itching to take flight. Itching to sting.

He glanced at the bulletproof facemask on the floorboard of his broken-down Civic and thought about leaving it behind. "Bulletproof" was a misnomer for that Chinese piece of junk. Leon knew from his research that the mask couldn't even stop a 9mm, much less a rifle round. But he picked it up anyway and slid the straps over his shaved head. It might not stop a bullet, but it would scare the shit out of the students soon to catch one themselves. That much it would do.

Across the parking lot of Willow Heights High School, a school resource officer was walking to his car. Leon slid lower in his seat, but between the distance and the tint on his windows, he doubted he had anything to worry about. It wasn't like they carried guns anyway. It would be quite a while—compared to how fast a semi-auto fired, at least—before the cops with guns showed up.

He'd parked close to the front entrance so that the walk to the door would be as short as possible. Willow Heights didn't employ automated access controls, but the doors did have locks that could be turned if someone spotted him in the parking lot and sounded the alarm. If the plan he'd spent months perfecting was going to fail, that would be its breakpoint. Having suffered more injustice the past twenty-five years of life than any person ought to, Leon's heart ached at the thought.

He checked his digital watch, then he creaked open the door of his car and stepped out into the icy November air. Despite the urgency of the situation, he stopped for a heartbeat to breathe in the moment. Willow Heights High School, with its cinder-block walls and chain link fences, looked more like a prison than a place of education. For Leon, that's exactly what it had been. He'd dropped out six years ago in 2005 after trying and failing for a second time to finish his senior year with passing grades. But time had done nothing to salve the wounds he'd suffered there. The bullying and the beatings. The rumors and the way the girls—the pretty ones and the not-so-pretty ones, too—would turn their noses up anytime he passed.

None of those classmates of his who had made his life hell—who had destroyed his self-esteem and prevented him from reaching his potential the way crabs in a bucket will pull each other down anytime one tries to escape—went to school there anymore. They'd all moved on to their idyllic adult lives. Got married. Got jobs. Had kids. Bought houses. And Leon could guarantee that none of them ever lost a wink of sleep over the life they'd ruined.

Well, he was about to make them care. It wouldn't be their blood he spilled, but they'd still get the message.

He took a deep breath. His heart was pounding. His hands were shaking so hard that the rifle shook, too. He realized this was the last chance to change his mind. To turn around and go back home. Or to fire just one shot instead of hundreds and take just one life today. Then he gritted his teeth and took the first step across the parking lot toward the school's front entrance.

The ice and snow crunched beneath his combat boots. The double glass doors he approached were closed. But they were not locked. Leon flung them open and stepped into the tile halls.

For the last four months, he had planned this day down to the minute. It was 11:52 a.m., which meant that the fifth bell had rung just two minutes ago. Students were crowding the hallways to get to their next class. Others, those who had early lunch, poured out of the cafeteria. The moment he opened the doors, Leon stepped into a target-rich environment.

He stood there unmoving for a moment. A few students noticed him and stared, too confused at first to be afraid. Leon caught eyes with one of them, a Hispanic kid wearing a baseball cap and an Abercrombie shirt.

Leon gritted his teeth. He would have screamed if dysfunctional vocal cords had not been yet another misery life saw fit to hand him at birth. Then he shouldered his rifle and began to fire.

Each shot was deafening. The screams and panicked footfalls were barely audible over the earsplitting explosions that came one after another without a half second between them. Leon fired into the mass of students without really aiming. Plenty of bodies were dropping anyway.

Those who weren't dead or dying had mostly scattered by the time Leon emptied his first magazine. A few students were lying flat on the floor with their hands covering their ears, shaking and bawling. A few more were cowering underneath the cafeteria tables. Leon hurried to reload before these stragglers came to their senses and fled, his veins coursing with adrenaline.

This was revenge at its heart, but it was more than that, too. It wasn't revenge that'd made him erect every time he daydreamed of this moment, that was making him even more erect now that the moment was here. He'd always been sick. Under different circumstances, a different school and a different upbringing, he might have stopped at killing toads and baby rabbits as a teenager. But there was no going back now, and nor did he want to.

One by one, he picked off the students who'd stuck around in the cafeteria. He took his time with these shots now that the crowd had parted, centering his reticle on the backs of their heads before carefully squeezing off a round.

A few more fiery barks and only one of them was left. She had stood up from underneath one of the far tables when the head of the boy next to her turned to confetti, but she didn't run. She wiped the blood and bits of scalp from her face, then turned to face Leon with eyes as wide and empty as craters on the moon.

Leon recognized her. Her name was Farrah Gosling, Bryan Gosling's little sister. Bryan, unlike most at this school, had always treated Leon kindly. Leon didn't know his sister very well, but he'd seen the two of them together after school. Bryan had always waited for her outside the junior high school building, then they would walk to the bus together. She had waved at Leon once, then blushed a little after. Even though she'd been much too young for him, it had made Leon's day. She didn't look so young anymore, though. Through the magnified scope, he could see a pair of full breasts just beneath his crosshairs.

Let her live, a voice soft and strangely feminine whispered in his head. It almost cut through. But the rush of everything else going through his mind was like whitewater, roiling and deafening and whisking him away.

Leon pulled the trigger twice. Farrah crumpled to the ground.

He took a moment to survey the scene. Bodies littered the cafeteria, balled up on the floor and slumped over tables. Most were still leaking blood onto the tile. Leon could hear it dripping. Could smell its old pennies scent in the air. He took a deep breath in through his nose to savor it, then he turned and ran for the exit doors.

If he'd kept hunting, started down the hallways and went

classroom to classroom, he probably could have killed many more. But his message had been sent. More to the point, the cops would be arriving soon. Leon had no desire to go out in a hail of bullets, where the risk of mere injury and subsequent capture was just as likely as a quick death. One well-placed bullet, on his own terms, was how he wanted this story to end.

He'd half expected to see an army of squad cars when he opened the doors, but the parking lot was empty. He could hear sirens wailing in the distance, though. He tossed the rifle into a bush near the entrance, then took off sprinting toward the dense woods behind the school.

It didn't take him long to reach them, but his pace slowed considerably when he crossed the tree line. The sirens were much closer now, probably screeching onto Evans Street, he figured. Leon took a few more crashing steps into the forest, far enough that no one would easily spot him from the school, then slumped down at the base of a pine tree.

He dug his fingers into the leafy soil and tried to steady his breathing. He'd meant for these last few moments to be spent in tranquility, with the sunlight filtering through the leaves and the cold, earthy breeze against his skin. But his adrenaline wouldn't allow it. Not even here in the one place that had always brought him a semblance of peace.

Leon had been the outdoorsy type since childhood. His high school job as a farm hand had kept him outside a lot, but he'd spent most of his off hours there, too. Fishing and canoeing and hunting crows. He'd killed so many crows, in fact, that it earned him a new nickname from the other farm hands. One he'd actually been fond of until the demons at Willow Heights High caught wind of it and turned it into something cruel.

You know they call you that because you've got straw for brains, right? Hank Bishop, one of the worst offenders, had said one day.

Well, Leon was going to prove that false, at least. He slid his Glock from its holster and racked the slide. He pushed it into his mouth until the barrel touched his palate, then lifted his eyes to the forest canopy. A crow circled overhead. Leon wondered if, by focusing on it hard enough, he might come back as that crow when he died.

His finger touched the gun's trigger, but before he could squeeze it, a noise somewhere behind him made him stop. It was a voice. A woman's voice.

And it was singing.

Even though the tune was faint and far away, Leon had never heard anything so mesmerizing. It entranced him in an instant. He rose in a daze, balancing himself against the pine tree, and let the Glock slip from his hands.

He saw no sign of the woman singing when he peered around the tree, but there was something else there, a little deeper into the forest, that caught his full attention.

It was a dirt road, right there in the middle of the woods. Next to it, the woods gave way to fields of corn. Leon could see ribbons of the yellow stalks through the trees and brambles.

He rubbed his eyes to make sure they weren't playing tricks on him. He'd ventured into these woods enough times to blaze up or ditch class that he knew there wasn't a road there. And there sure as hell wasn't any cornfield. Not here, on this tiny little strip of land, smack dab in the middle of town.

Such logic no longer mattered, though. He couldn't hear the woman singing anymore, but the road still called to him just as powerfully. Smiling, panting, feeling suddenly as drunk as the first time he tried liquor, Leon stumbled toward it.

CHAPTER SIX

"There's a pillow and blankets on the bed already," Benjamin said. "Haven't been washed in years, but no one's slept on them in years neither. You don't seem like the type to care anyway." He went into the kitchen, then returned with a kerosene lantern, this one a little smaller than the two big ones he used to light the living room.

"Take this in case you need to find your way around. I don't need you bumping into things and waking me up. There's an outhouse just outside the back door and a pitcher of water in the kitchen. You shouldn't have no reason to be wandering around anywhere else in the middle of the night, and that includes the pantry. I'm willing to share with those who pull their weight—which is quite a lot in your case—but you eat what I give you and nothing more. We aren't exactly living high on the hog here. Food has to be made to last."

He studied Jason in the lantern light. He'd been studying him all night, but there wasn't a lot to go off of. The fellow seemed to treat words the same way Benjamin treated the food stores: like he was going to run out of them someday.

He sure didn't mind letting his fists do the talking, though. For the sake of expedience, Benjamin had let it slide. But that was nowhere near the same as forgiveness.

"Why doesn't this place have plumbing?" Jason asked. "Or electricity, for that matter."

"Do I look like a rich man to you? Does this farm look like a mansion in the city?"

"Everywhere has electricity."

"Maybe where you're from." Benjamin was glad when he didn't probe further. Some threads didn't need to be pulled on too hard just yet.

Over the past hour, he'd told Jason as much as he needed to know. About the five Avengers, what they looked like, their common paths and territories around the farm, their favorite ways to ruin your day.

What he hadn't told him was how they got there. That they'd arrived here just like him— that they used to be normal flesh and blood just like him, too—was the part Benjamin could never let him find out.

"I've got a rooster that always crows at first light. If that doesn't wake you up, I'll be in to do it myself. We've got a lot of work to get done tomorrow, and like I told you earlier—"

"If I'm going to eat your food, I have to pull my weight."

"Your *substantial* weight, mind you."

"I'm not afraid of hard work."

"That's good," Benjamin said. "It's the least of the things you have to be afraid of now."

Jason took the lantern from him without another word and disappeared down the hall. Benjamin watched him until he sank into the shadows. He heard the bedroom door open, then heard the latch close.

He didn't go to bed himself until quite some time later. There was too much thinking to do. A dangerous game had begun the moment Jason showed up at the farm. For Benjamin, the only way to win was to make sure he never found out the rules.

CHAPTER SEVEN

Jason flicked his hands and sent a spray of blood onto the grass. He wiped the sweat from his forehead with his upper sleeve to keep from smearing his face, then he went back to work.

It wasn't his first time chopping up a body. However, it was the first time the body belonged to a goat. And definitely the first time he'd been required to chop one up so precisely.

"No, damn you," Benjamin hissed. "You're still leaving way too much meat on the bone." He took the knife from Jason's hand and elbowed him to the side. "Put your knife flat against the shoulder blade and work it down nice and even-like. Like this." He peeled a ragged strip from the mangle of flesh Jason had left behind and waggled it in front of his face. "Won't be good for nothing but stew meat now. Hell, everything you've carved off so far looks like it's already been chewed on, son."

Benjamin handed the knife back to him with a huff. Jason imagined prying open the old man's mouth and fisting it down his throat, handle and all.

He couldn't kill him here, not permanently, anyway, but there were other options. He could chain him up. Hobble him.

Remove his arms and legs, cauterize the stumps, then drag him around by the neck like a dead dog on a leash.

It made for a nice daydream. There was only one problem with the idea: without the old man, Jason would starve.

His experience with farming ended at growing a sunflower for middle-school science class and playing Farmville. Until he figured out some solution, resisting his violent urges was Jason's only option. And that was something he had about as much experience with as farming.

"You got to get the lead out, son. Hot as it is out here, this meat won't be fit for the damn hogs if we don't get it curing quick."

Jason glared at him. "Do you want it done fast or do you want it done right?"

"Hell, I'd settle for either one at this point," Benjamin shot back. "Just start carrying what we got so far into the curing shed. It's that small building behind the house. You ought to be able to manage that, I think."

Jason picked up a wooden crate brimming with flesh and bone and tried to ignore the way it whetted his appetite. Not his appetite for food, but for turning that smart-mouthed old asshole into a similar heap of gore.

It took him a while to transport all the crates of meat from the butcher table in the barn to the curing shed. Outside the shade, the sun was nearly unbearable, and by the time he was done, his face was flushed. The seething he felt inside, however, had cooled some by then.

"One more job for you," Benjamin said. "I need you to drag this carcass to the pond and toss it in. At least all the meat you left behind will make fine food for the catfish."

"I need to rest a minute," Jason said. He'd expected pushback, but the old man must have seen the shade of his skin. Jason sat down on a barrel near the wall and took a long gulp from his canteen. "So, is this how it's going to be every time?" he asked once he'd wetted his throat.

"How what's going to be every time?"

"Me busting my ass doing all the grunt work while you sit there and bitch at me."

"Son, every operation needs two things to be successful: brains and brawn. We both know damn well where you slot in." Benjamin watched him for a second, then grinned, exposing more gums than teeth. "You look like you're about to have a heatstroke. Or an aneurism maybe. You'd pop right back up anyway even if you did. But hell, you just rest there a minute, son. Clearly, honest work don't suite you well."

He grabbed hold of the goat by its bloodstained horns, then slid it off the table. Jason watched it hit the dirt. The carcass was bare and limbless from the neck down—just a ribcage and spinal column, both grisly and dripping—but the head was still intact. It lolled to the side when it landed so that one of its glazed brown eyes seemed to be looking right at Jason.

"What happens to the livestock?" Jason asked.

"What are you talking about?"

"Do they come back, too?"

"No. And that means we have to manage the herds carefully. I used to enjoy a nice turkey dinner sometimes. Was one of my favorites...until the last hen died about fifteen years ago. You don't take care of them, you don't breed 'em just right and choose which ones you slaughter carefully, and it's gonna be another meat off the menu from here on out."

"How do you know which ones to slaughter?" To Benjamin, it probably sounded like small talk. Jason had no interest in small talk, but agriculture interested him greatly now; the more he learned, the less his life would depend on the old man.

"I just pick the ones that look at me funny." Benjamin grinned at his own joke despite being the only one, then he began dragging the goat carcass out of the barn, leaving a snail trail of blackish blood in the dirt. "Catch your breath," he said on his way out. "We got to weed the vegetable garden when I get back. And the goat pen has a couple loose wires that need to be re-stretched. The sneaky devils keep getting out and dropping pellets in my yard."

Jason watched him drag the goat out of the barn and down the hill outside. There was a small pond in the valley at the bottom. The grade was steep enough that he couldn't see it from where he sat, but he'd seen it earlier. It was stocked with catfish and sunfish, according to Benjamin—both of which were fine eating, also according to Benjamin. Jason didn't care much for fish, but he would've eaten just about anything at the moment. Breakfast had been meager—a slice of tomato, a thin slice of ham, and two boiled eggs—and they hadn't stopped for lunch. Now it was pushing 3 o'clock, and Jason's stomach was starting to ache. The rationing didn't make much sense to him given the abundance of livestock and crops he'd seen so far. It made him resent the old man that much more.

There were about two dozen goats that roamed a fenced-in section of pasture behind the house, and next to the barn was a large pig pen with almost as many pigs. Chickens roamed the property freely, and Jason had seen a lot of them, too. Then there was the fishpond, and the vegetable garden, and the trio of fruit trees in the front yard. That's not to mention the cornfield that seemed to stretch on forever (and, according to Benjamin, *did*).

And yet the greedy old man harped on about rations and fed him meals hardly large enough to dull the ache.

Three days he'd spent here so far. Three days of grueling work, insufferable company, and total sobriety. That last one didn't make much sense to Jason either; surely an old-timer like Benjamin Parker knew how to turn corn into whiskey.

Nothing like what happened on the road with The Scarecrow had happened again so far. *The Flip,* Benjamin called it.

"Seems like the place is easing you in nice and gentle-like", he'd said this morning after another night of normalcy came and went. Jason still couldn't completely shake the instinct that it was all bullshit, but then he'd remember the way the old man's caved-in face had pieced itself back together. Seeing that had been even more convincing to him than his own death and resurrection; what happened to him on the road still defied his understanding, but he understood what it meant to beat someone to death.

No dream nor drug could explain how the old man came back from that.

When Jason had cooled enough that his head was no longer spinning, he rose from his seat on the barrel and walked slowly across the barn. All manner of tools hung on its peeling walls. He recognized some of the more common ones—shovels and hoes and posthole diggers—but others were foreign to him. Some of them were so rusted it looked like they hadn't been taken off the wall in ages. Jason let his fingers slide across the dangling line of wooden handles as he walked, jostling the tools against the pegs they hung from and not so accidentally knocking a couple from the wall.

His fingers stopped on an item he recognized right away, but one seemingly out of place amidst all the farm tools. It was a pair of iron shackles, rusted a little on the links but still thick and strong. Touching the shackles, despite these being much more a tool of his trade than the rest of those on the wall, made Jason's skin prickle. He dropped his hand to his side and kept moving.

There was a hayloft near the end of the barn with a wooden ladder leading up to it. Jason thought about climbing up and taking a nap on the straw. He thought, too, about how quickly the whole place would flare up if he tossed a match into the loft. Then he lost interest in the hay and exited the barn.

His eyes followed the trail of blood and flattened grass down the hill outside the barn. It ended at the pond bank where the old man stood. Jason watched him heave the carcass into the water, a faint splash carrying on the wind.

The catfish must have been used to this routine. Soon, the water was churning with gray-blue fins as they twisted and tore at their gory meal. Jason found himself wishing he'd gone with the old man to get a closer look, and he started down the hill.

The slope was relatively gentle—far from a straight drop. Yet his first step down the hill made Jason's breath catch. It felt like stepping off a mountain ledge.

His insides flopped, and his legs gave out. He hit the ground with his hands outstretched to keep from rolling, then heard a piercing, familiar sound. Like rusted steel grinding against itself. The earsplitting whine seemed to come from inside his head. Dots speckled his vision like sparks from the metal's friction, and he could almost taste the steel on his tongue.

The temperature dropped. The sun vanished, and a million blood-red stars took its place in a now jet-black sky. Once again, it seemed like the whole world turned—not in the normal way, but in a way he could feel in the pit of his stomach. Like gravity ceased to exist for an instant.

This time, when the brief vertigo passed, Jason was quick to his feet. He spun around, scanning for any immediate threats, but saw nothing except the waist-high grass that was now dry and dead and rippling against a cold wind.

Jason turned his attention to the bottom of the hill, scanning the pond bank where the old man had been. But he wasn't there anymore. The water shone green in the strange moonlight, and a heavy fog rose from its surface. Both the pond and the sagging cattails at its edges were completely undisturbed.

A noise behind him, from the barn, made Jason freeze. A sharp clattering, like a tool falling from its pegs on the wall. He heard breathing from somewhere within the barn's black mouth, so deep and labored it was audible over the wind, then the eager whine of a dog.

Not waiting another instant, Jason barreled down the hill. He tripped once in the darkness, rolled a bit, and banged his shoulder against a rock, but he scrambled back to his feet and kept going.

The old man had to still be somewhere nearby. If there was any safety to be found here, it was with him. Jason lurched to a halt at the edge of the pond bank, just where the ground began to soften into mud, and swept his eyes across the water. He'd thought that maybe the old man had dove in when The Flip happened, but if he was hiding somewhere in the dark reeds along the bank, then Jason had no chance of spotting him.

"*Benjamin*," he hissed as loud as he dared. "*Where the fuck are you?*"

There was no reply from the stagnant water. But up the hill, a pack of dogs began to bray. Their deep howls and wet, snapping barks carried strangely through the misty air in a way that made Jason's hairs stand on end.

He quickly considered his options. Run was what panicked instinct begged for him to do, but Jason let logic prevail; there wasn't a sprinter alive who could outrun a juiced-up pack of dogs. That left hiding as his only option. And there was only one place to do it.

He dropped to his belly at the edge of the pond and sank his fingers into the mud beneath the shallow water. Doing his best not to make a splash, he dragged himself into the pond. It was cold enough to shock his nerves and reeked of must and sulfur, but he pulled himself deeper, clawing his way along the mucky bottom until it was deep enough for him to slip beneath the surface.

He avoided opening his eyes in the foul water, and it wouldn't have mattered if he did; it was so dark and murky that even just a few feet down not a ray of moonlight cut through. But the far bank was just a stone's throw away, and the reeds on that side were taller. He wasn't sure how long he'd be able to hide there before hypothermia set in, but it was the only plan he had for now.

Jason surfaced just as his lungs began to burn; the thought of inhaling the grimy water sent fear into his muscles. Had it been so rancid before The Flip? Jason thought back to the catfish in the shimmering, blue water and knew that it had not.

The bank was close. The water was likely shallow enough now that he could have stood, but he stayed flat with only his head and shoulders above the surface. There was a small depression in the embankment with thin roots and strings of algae hanging over it like curtains. Jason pushed them aside and wedged himself into the crevice.

The dogs were close now, just across the pond near the spot he'd entered the water by the sound of it. He heard the whines and snarls of at least three of the beasts, no doubt frustrated that the scent trail they'd been following had ended. With just his eyes and nose above the water, Jason tried to make them out and could only see their silhouettes darting back and forth along the bank.

That and another dark form coming down the hill. This one tall and plodding. A piercing whistle quieted every dog in the pack and stilled their frantic movements. Jason held his breath.

"Boy!"

In the silence so eerie that not even the crickets and frogs dared break it, the figure's voice sounded booming. *Strange* and booming.

"Come forth, boy!"

Jason was going to do no such thing. But he also didn't know how much longer he could stay in the water. His fingers and arms were starting to tingle. His legs had already moved past that phase and were now completely numb. It confounded him how the water had turned so cold. Before The Flip, it would've been the perfect day for a swim.

Slowly, still keeping as much of himself as he could underwater, Jason poked his head out of the crevice and scanned his escape routes. In both directions, the pond bank was tall and steep. He'd have to pull himself up at first until the ground leveled, and there'd be no way to do it quickly. Or quietly.

Something jerked his attention back to the far bank. Or the *lack of something*, rather. The tall figure was gone. The dogs, too, unless they were all lying perfectly still in the grass. Jason strained his eyes to see if he could spot any of them amidst the shadowy weeds, but weeds and water were all that the dim, yellow moonlight revealed.

He thought about making a break for it while maybe he still had a chance. His mind was racing through his options when the sound of a heavy boot thudding into the soil above his head silenced all thought.

Steadily, quietly, Jason filled his lungs with air and eased beneath the water. Making it back to the other side of the pond on a breath hold was his only chance. He wasn't sure his frozen muscles were up to the task.

As it went, he never got the chance to find out. Just a single butterfly stroke was all Jason managed before the still surface above his head erupted and a rough, thick hand grabbed him by the hair. His pursuer hoisted him out of the water like a fish on a hook, setting his scalp on fire as the skin stretched and ripped under his weight. Water and slime dripped from his body and left ripples like raindrops beneath his dangling feet.

"*There ye are, boy!*" The monster holding him with a single, outstretched arm like a kitten held by its scruff bellowed so loud it made Jason's ears ring. A wad of something wet and cold flew from the thing's mouth and landed on his cheek, reeking of dental rot and tobacco.

Jason lifted his eyes to behold the abomination. The skin of its face was bone-white and sagged like the jowls of a bloodhound. Its teeth were made of wood and lead and ivory all jumbled together and rooted in rotting, gray gums. Only a few greasy, black strands of the thing's real hair poked out from underneath the powdered wig it wore. Jason could see an army of little brown bugs scuttling through the wig's chalky wool.

He darted his disbelieving eyes up and down, surveying the rest of the giant, rotting absurdity that held him by the hair. He saw a dark-gray coat, moldy and spotted with moth holes. Pointed shoes with rusted buckles. Frills of stiff, stained lace around every hem on the thing's attire. And all of these attached to a frame that must have stood eight feet tall.

Then Jason saw the earth traveling towards him as the Colonial Era nightmare spiked his head into the dirt. Just before darkness enveloped him, one of Benjamin's many warnings flashed across his mind.

Whatever you do, don't let The Slaver catch you alive.

Samuel's Transgression

Samuel Taylor was a man who never neglected to count his blessings. In fact, counting them was one of his favorite things to do. Two hundred and eleven acres of pristine Virginia soil was the first of their number, a thriving plantation where, during the growing season, over half a million tobacco plants lifted their leaves to the sun. Along with these, he owned eleven horses, three houses on the property and another in the city, three carriages, nine mules, fifty-four head of cattle...

And one hundred and thirteen human beings.

Not that he considered them such. In Samuel's eyes, the Negro condition was one with a single, simple cure: absolute subjugation to the superior race. Thus was their natural order in the world. Their predestined role in God's perfect design.

If ever accused (though no one ever did), he would have balked at the notion that he hated their kind. Samuel hated Negroes no more than he hated swine and cattle. And he treated them just the same.

Mostly the same, at least. As a subhuman race, they existed in the cloudy space between beast and man. They could be cunning, no doubt about that. And determined. And rebellious. These characteristics required much more persistence to curb than what it took to break a horse or train a dog to obey. Over the years, Samuel had perfected his process, learning first from the mistakes of his father and the issues his gentle hand created, then eventually from his own experience after Father died and the plantation became his to manage. Like bread baked without enough yeast to rise, there'd been far too little of one key ingredient in Father's recipe for handling the slaves: suffering.

What Samuel had found was that the higher level functionings of humanity could not exist in a state of constant agony. One cannot dream of freedom when they are too tormented to sleep, and food is the only ambition of the starving.

This approach did have its drawbacks, though. Drawbacks that an honest man like himself could not deny. Breakage was its biggest con. He had become a fixture at the Richmond slave market since taking over the plantation, constantly having to replace those that couldn't make the cut. Or, in a more literal sense the times when he got carried away—a not uncommon occurrence—couldn't *survive the cuts*.

Runaways were another issue with his methods. Though, in a business sense, this was a form of breakage, too. Albeit the worst kind of all. Samuel might not have hated the Negroes, at least by his own definitions, but he despised runaways. Nothing made him hotter than the shame of letting one of *them* get the better of him. The loss of property was an afterthought in comparison; more times than not, those he caught ended up perishing from their punishment regardless.

Only a handful had ever managed to make it far. Between the hounds and the small army of farmhands and mercenaries from town he brought to bear, the odds were always stacked against them. Samuel never took any chances with runaways, but he liked to think he could have captured most of them even without so many eyes and noses searching the woods. What he'd never dare admit aloud to the men in his hunting club (to whom, after too many rounds of rye whiskey, he admitted most things) was that Samuel could *think* like a Negro. He had lived alongside them his entire life. He had studied them. Bred with them. Watched them die. Though it was a mostly unprovable thing, he swore it made his instincts for catching them when they ran sharp as a tack.

Except now, it grew more likely by the minute that his instincts—and the hounds and those blundering fools for hire, too—were going to fail him. The dogs had led them deep into the forest south of his plantation, probably three or four miles past its border. And now, just as the sun was starting to set, the worthless mutts had lost the trail.

One of the bloodhounds was sniffing in circles around Samuel's feet, turning up leaves with its broad, black nose. Samuel eyed it with contempt, then kicked it hard in the ribs. Hearing its bawls, the rest of the dogs lifted their snouts from the ground to stare for a moment at their wounded comrade before picking the search back up again with seemingly more fervor than before.

"What ails thy hounds, Samuel?" asked a tall, gaunt man named Edward Smith. He was one of the plantation's overseers and a man whom Samuel trusted, though just now the sound of his voice made Samuel's head buzz.

"Nothing. They be the finest hounds in all the colonies."

"Then why canst they catch the scent?"

Samuel scowled. Weather was the problem—both the winds that drove hard from the south and carried the scent away from them and the rain that washed it from the leaves and soil. The slave named Jupiter had chosen his opportunity well. Cunning, they could be. Cunning like a fox.

Samuel looked up to the angry, gray-green skies that showed no sign of stilling their fury. Then he bowed his head and closed his eyes as if to pray. He took a deep breath of the petrichor air and let the sounds of dogs scurrying about and raindrops splashing fade away. In his mind's ears, he could hear Jupiter's voice now. The way its warm tenor sounded when he sang hymns and work songs. Samuel pictured his face—the curve of his jawline, the lines on his forehead, the small scar on his cheek shaped like a scythe blade. He willed himself inside the runaway's mind, straining to hear his fearful thoughts from somewhere in these woods. Straining so hard and so literally to picture what the slave was seeing—what he was thinking, what he planned—that the muscles in Samuel's face began to cramp.

"It would be wise to retrace our steps. Perchance the hounds will—"

"Hold thy tongue, Edward," Samuel commanded without lifting his head. He focused on his meditations for a few moments longer, then looked up and opened his eyes. "Take the hounds and set thy course for the west."

"Where shall you go?"

"Just do as I bid."

Edward obeyed without further question. Samuel watched him and the dogs until they vanished into the trees, then he went searching for a tree of his own. He found what he was looking for not but a few paces away: a tall maple with branches well-distributed, and some low enough to the ground for him to reach the first rung. He grabbed hold of one and hoisted himself up. The bark scraped at his forearms, but his cold-numbed skin hardly felt the pain. Like going up a disjointed ladder, Samuel climbed the tree until he was near the top—high enough up that he could see a much larger area of forest than before. He looped his arm around the base of a branch for support and waited.

What he'd told Edward had been no lie. His dogs were the finest in all the colonies. They never lost the scent of a runaway, rain or no rain. If they were leading them in circles, then the reason was clear: just like his namesake, Jupiter was traveling in circles, too.

On the surface, it wasn't a terrible plan. He must have been hoping that his pursuers would grow tired of following the dogs on what seemed like a goose chase and eventually retrace their steps, just as Edward, that fool, had suggested. It would have given him all the time he needed to disappear into the wilderness for good. To make it to one of the maroon communities or Indian tribes, if he could survive that long. Or to at least die a free man if not. Well, Samuel thought, almost giddy with himself, that was not going to happen.

He debated what he'd do with Jupiter once he was captured. Death would be the final outcome, that much was a given; he had to set an example for the rest, and it wasn't like he'd be losing much anyway. Jupiter was probably the weakest male slave in Samuel's stock, a runt of a man whom Samuel never would have paid good coin for at auction. But he'd been born on the plantation to a slave who'd been pregnant at purchase, and he had worked even harder than the rest every day since to make up for his feebleness just enough to keep Samuel from culling him.

If it'd been Moses or Titus who he was hunting, Samuel would've been double-checking the powder in his flintlock pistols to make sure it was dry. As it were, he planned to drop right down on top of scrawny little Jupiter whenever he circled back around again. Pin him, shackle him, and drag him back alive.

From there, the possibilities were endless. Samuel had culled his livestock in a lot of creative ways, but he had never flayed one of them before. He'd read accounts of flayings from the Dark Ages and found the idea intriguing. He wondered if he might be able to do it so skillfully, so precisely, that Jupiter could be sent back out into the field to toil in the dust and sun one final time with every nerve ending in his body exposed.

Just then, a sound from somewhere in the woods pulled Samuel from his daydreams. He perked his ears, then furrowed his brow as the sound became clearer. It wasn't branches snapping or the panting of exhausted prey. It was singing. Not a man's voice either, but a woman's.

Little by little, Samuel's confusion morphed into intrigue. He had never married, had never had much use for the weaker sex. Just one use, really, and the slave girls had met that need adequately ever since he turned fourteen. But the way the song carried on the wind, the way the rain and thunder seemed to become a part of its rhythm, took him back even further than this. Back to when he was a wrinkly babe latched to his mother's breast, before the cholera took her. He'd been so young when she passed that he'd never been able to picture her face, but he could picture it clearly now. She smiled at him. Her hair shined like copper in the sunlight, her eyes were like those of a fawn, and it seemed now that the song which had become clear as crystal in his ears was coming from her lips. In a stupor of longing and childlike wonder, Samuel began to shimmy down the tree.

His feet had no sooner touched the ground when he spotted the road. Seeing it there as if it had been there all along should have been the most confounding experience of his life. But Samuel just smiled and wiped the tears from his eyes as he stumbled toward it.

The rain stopped the moment his boots touched the road's gravel. The skies cleared, and the air turned warm. Fields of corn stretched in every direction. Even in the direction he'd come from. Samuel would have noticed this if he'd ever stopped and turned around to see the forest he'd just exited gone as though it had never been there in the first place. But he didn't look back.

There was a building at the end of the road that looked quite strange even from a distance. It appeared to be a home, though not one similar to any Samuel had ever seen before. The materials were unusual, the boards of the walls too straight and symmetrical, the windows too large and numerous. Yet all of these oddities only enchanted him more.

He saw someone outside the home. A man probably ten or fifteen years his elder wearing the strangest-looking clothing that Samuel had ever laid eyes on: bright blue trousers with a bib in the front that covered the chest and straps of the same odd material looped over the shoulders.

The man looked up and noticed him then. Over the sound of a song that had already started to fade, Samuel heard his curses filling the air.

CHAPTER EIGHT

Taste was the first of Jason's senses to return. A cocktail of blood and dirt in his mouth that made him gag and spit. Rain drenched his skin—his exposed skin, for he realized then that he wasn't wearing a scrap of clothing. Not unless you count the shackles he felt clamped around his wrists and ankles and the thick chains connecting them. This brought him fully awake in an instant, his eyes flashing open.

He was lying face down in the mud. A lone ant made ripples as it thrashed in a puddle just in front of his nose. A second later, he saw the same pair of old, brass-buckled boots he'd seen earlier step into view.

He felt them next. The right one at least, crashing hard into his midsection. Driving the air from his chest. Jason coughed, then tried to stop coughing when it flared the pain in his side. Hard to say right away before the bruise had even formed, but it might have broken ribs.

"*Rise,*" said a voice like a death-rattle. Fearing another kick, Jason obeyed. He struggled at first to find his footing in the waterlogged ground, slipping back to his hands and knees before finally managing to straighten his wobbly legs.

Even standing, Jason had to lift his head to see The Slaver's face. A poor decision, it turned out. One met with a backhand so violent it spun his head and knocked him back down to the ground.

"How dare thou meet my gaze, slave! Now rise!"

Jason stood again, keeping his eyes on the ground this time. His ears were ringing, and his left cheek was stinging and warm.

"Walk," the harsh, ghostly voice demanded. Without looking up to see where he was going, Jason began to walk.

The Slaver circled behind him, but a blow to the back of the head the first time he tried to lift his eyes told Jason he still wasn't allowed to do so. He marched blindly through the rain and mud, the chains around his feet forcing him to measure each step. Eventually, the walls and door of a crude wooden building came into view, though Jason nearly ran into it before he saw it.

"Open the door."

There was a padlock hanging from the bolt, but it wasn't latched. The bolt screeched as Jason turned it. He pushed open the door a crack, then made the mistake of pausing.

A boot to the small of his back slammed him into the door and flung it open the rest of the way. Jason tumbled to the plank floor and reached out his shackled hands to break his fall. His palms slid across the crumbling planks, and a large splinter buried itself into his skin.

Before he could stand, The Slaver knelt and grabbed hold of the chain connecting his arms. Jason noticed a thick, iron hitching ring drilled into the floor, then a second later he was fastened to it with a padlock that seemed to have appeared from nowhere into The Slaver's meaty hand.

The boards creaked beneath his thudding steps as The Slaver stood and walked behind Jason to the other side of the room. Jason lifted his eyes just enough to see the wall in front of him. It was made of uneven timbers, old and graying with a few scraggly strips of bark still clinging to some of them. Little natural light entered the windowless space, but the walls were aglow in the red-orange tone of firelight. He heard something stirring the coals, and the glow flared brighter.

"Hold still."

Jason, who had spoken these words enough times to his own victims to know that pain was coming next, focused on the floor and clenched his teeth.

Pressure on the side of his thigh was the first thing he felt. He heard the sizzle of his skin searing before he felt it, as though it took a beat for his nerves to get out the message. Then that message came through loud and clear.

Jason screamed through gritted teeth. Spit, tears, and snot all splattered the floor beneath his face. When the blazing steel finally lifted from his flesh, he squirmed onto his bare buttocks and took stock of the damage. The skin on his thigh was reddening and blistering right before his eyes, bringing the crisp shape of the wound into clearer focus: a letter S wound around a letter T like a snake on a rod.

"No thieves shall steal my property," The Slaver croaked as if offering explanation.

Just as Jason began to make sense of what was happening, the brand came down again. The Slaver shoved it into his stomach this time, right above the groin. Jason tried to scream again, but he'd strained his voice so much already that only a raspy gurgle came out. He tried to writhe away, but the minimal slack in his chains left him nowhere to go. The brand lifted, only a few inches this time, then came down again on his chest.

"Gaaaah! Fucking stop!"

The Slaver raised the brand in front of his drooping face, inspecting it with milky eyes. The metal had cooled to a dull shade of orange. A small piece of skin was stuck to the top of it, sizzling like a strip of bacon. "*Needs to be reheated*," he muttered to himself as he trudged back to the firepit.

Four times. Four times more the monster reheated the brand in the fire and cooled it against Jason's skin before he mercifully passed out from the pain.

Relieved the livestock was no longer writhing and making such a fuss, The Slaver stood back and appraised his work. Then he reheated the brand yet again and set about marking all the spots he'd missed.

CHAPTER NINE

Plagued by nightmares throughout his youth, Jason Baker knew well the feeling of relief when you wake and realize it was only a dream. Not that the waking world had ever been a paradise for him, but at least it made sense.

Now, the experience had been flipped. The time he'd spent unconscious had been marked by all manner of feverish dreams, yet none of them compared to the nightmare he woke to. As the horror of it set in, Jason fought to stay asleep. But clinging to the peaceful darkness was like trying to catch smoke in his hands.

His skin was on fire. It felt like every inch of it was engulfed with invisible flames. Struck by the thought that he was lying on a grill, he rolled to his side. The scrape of the wooden floor against his raw, blistered flesh made the pain even worse and caused Jason to cry out.

"*Thou hast woken.*" The voice came from across the room. Jason heard footsteps approaching, then jumped at the sudden clatter when a tin bowl hit the floor beside him. "*Eat.*"

Half the bowl's contents—an off-white sludge that Jason didn't recognize—slopped out onto the ground. He wouldn't have felt like eating if it had been buttered lobster, but he didn't need a demonstration to know what refusal would get him.

Jason expected it to taste like vomit, but the porridge had hardly any flavor at all. It wasn't until he noticed the first maggot halfway through the bowl that his stomach turned. He emptied the bowl anyway, watching the entire time from the corner of his eye as The Slaver twitched the end of a thick, black whip across the floor, seeming frustrated he'd been given no excuse to use it yet. Once only a few dregs of porridge and one dead maggot were left stuck to the bottom, Jason pushed the bowl aside.

"Eat!"

He was given no chance to figure out what this meant on his own before The Slaver grabbed him by the hair and pushed his face into the largest glob of spillage on the floor. Jason worked his mouth up and down, inhaling as much as he could manage with his nose smashed flat against the wood. When he choked and coughed most of it back up, The Slaver roared.

The whip came down against Jason's already ruined back, cutting a line across the dozens of letter-shaped burns. The pain was paralyzing. It sucked the breath from his lungs and left him unable to draw another.

"EAT!"

Some primal part of him took over then and did whatever was required to prevent more pain. The rest of his mind took refuge somewhere else. While his body slurped rotten porridge from the floor, his thoughts went to the school bus in seventh grade with Mrs. Jackson behind the wheel. Not a pleasant memory per se, but all the memories Jason considered pleasant were too brutal themselves for a retreat from pain and violence.

When the floor was licked clean, The Slaver stepped away and returned a few seconds later with a pail of water. "*Drink.*"

This, Jason did without hesitation. His throat felt like cracked clay, and the water, though warm, was clear and tasteless. He drank straight from the pail until it felt like his stomach was about to reject it. Panic flared as he thought of the punishment to come if that happened, and he forced the feeling to pass.

"*Rise.*"

Trembling and wobbling, Jason obeyed. With so many wounds demanding his nervous system's attention like hundreds of screaming babies, he didn't notice until he was standing that even the soles of his feet had been branded. Their screams rose to the forefront the moment he put weight on them, but Jason gritted through it.

He didn't dare lift his eyes. The Slaver's massive boots and the moldy hems of his trousers were all that Jason could see.

"*Thy learning is swift. A cunning one, art thou not?*"

Jason didn't answer, just kept his eyes locked on the floor.

"*I despise the cunning ones…tell me thy name.*"

He nearly lied on instinct, then felt horribly certain the monster would know somehow if he did. "Jason Baker."

"*Thy name is Jupiter now.*"

"Okay. Whatever you say. I'm Jupiter. If that's what—"

"*DAMNATION UPON THEE, JUPITER!*" The Slaver struck him across the face with the butt of the whip. Jason hit the floor hard. He felt a burn blister on his side burst beneath the impact.

"RISE!"

Again, some deeper functioning took over. His eyes stayed lowered to the floor when he managed to get back to his feet, but it wasn't the floor he was seeing. He saw trees passing by through a dusty window, the ripped seatback of a cloth bench, and the back of Sally Wiltshire's blonde head.

"Look at me." Jason hesitated for an instant, saw the whip rising again, then quickly lifted his head. The Slaver was standing just inches from him. Close enough for Jason to smell the rot wafting off his body. His clouded eyes were still and lifeless, yet clearly full of fury. The muscles in his sagging face shook, and he clenched his jaw so hard that Jason could hear the wood and metal and bone of his freakish dentures all grinding together. *"Look upon what thou hast done to me, Jupiter."*

Jason had no idea how to respond. No idea what was expected of him, or what would bring another lash of the whip. So he kept his mouth shut and his gaze blank.

"Juuuupiter. Damnation upon thee, Jupiter. Hellfire and DAMNATION!" Jason winced, fully expecting another strike. But The Slaver just towered over him, muscular limbs trembling with rage. His chest heaved beneath his soiled coat, forcing rancid breath down onto Jason's face. *"Tell me how thou did it, Jupiter. What pagan sorcery did thou use?"*

"I...I don't know..."

"LIAR! Wretched, pagan LIAR!" The whip snapped the ground

near Jason's feet, peeling up a sliver of wood from the floor.

"Fuck! Please, just...just fucking *please!*"

"What is thy name?"

"Jason...Jupiter, I mean. Fuck! Look, it's whatever you want it to be, alright?"

"Thou aren't Jupiter. Thy skin is too white. Thy soul is too black. Blaaaack as tar. Black as sin, and the judgment of sinners is nye, Jaaasooon Baaaaker. Thy *judgment is nye."*

"No more," Jason pleaded, his head lowered and shaking.

"Sleep." Then, a heartbeat later when Jason still hadn't moved: *"SLEEP!"*. Jason hit the deck and curled himself into a ball, clenching closed his red, dripping eyes.

He heard The Slaver's footsteps leaving the room, heard the building's only door open and close, then heard the screech and click of a rusty padlock latching.

Jupiter's Mission

On hands and knees, Jupiter stopped his work for a moment to lift his eyes skyward and dream of home. Not the home in Nigeria his mother had spoken of before her passing. Born on the Taylor plantation, Jupiter had never seen this homeland, though the stories she'd told had always filled him with wonder. The home he longed for now predated this heritage. Predated even the ancestral soil itself.

The path you've been chosen to walk will be challenging, he could remember a voice his soul missed deeply saying. *But your mission is holy. And your reward will be great.*

Though he would have done it all over again if given the choice, he'd been incredibly naïve back then. As a being who had never known toil and suffering since the first hour of its creation, how could he have possibly understood what "challenging" truly meant?

Twenty-six years of life on earth later and he knew the meaning intimately.

It had been difficult for him from life's first breath. He'd been a sickly child, small and weak and prone to illness. Yet his masters—first Henry Taylor, then eventually his much crueler son—had never seen this as cause to lighten his burden. As soon as he was old enough to walk, Jupiter had been put to work in the fields. From the first rays of dawn to the last glow of twilight, he would push his body to its limits and beyond to keep from falling behind. By the time he stood in line for the only meal of the day he'd be given, it took all his strength not to collapse to the floor.

These were the daily hardships, but there were always the days that would come along and drag his understanding of suffering to terrible new depths. The scars across his body told the story of these days, some dating back to his youth, others still fresh and scabbed over. Young Master Taylor had fallen in love with the whip the moment he first held one in his hands. And that was the most lenient of his punishments, reserved for minor offenses like slacking off or speaking out of turn. Jupiter counted himself blessed that he'd managed to avoid the worst of Samuel's sadism so far and thus still had all his body parts; there were plenty of gelded men and nine-fingered women on the Taylor plantation who had not been so fortunate.

And yet, dear Jupiter, he heard his friend's voice say, *would not even they count themselves blessed thanks to you?*

Jupiter stopped his work for a heartbeat, a bundle of tobacco leaves in one hand and a curved blade in the other. A thought so self-important would not have usually crossed his mind; sometimes he wondered if it really was her speaking to him, ministering to him from beyond while he ministered to those whose burden he'd been sent to lighten.

The Taylor plantation was an abomination. An insult to all that was good and holy. The men and women—the *children*—forced to suffer here lived lives more wretched than any being deserved, let alone children of God. So God sent them an angel.

Every slave on the property had felt it the moment Jupiter was born, a flourish in their crushed spirits, a newfound brightness to their days and peacefulness to their nights. The Taylor family and the plantation's overseers had felt it, too, though Jupiter imagined that, to them, it hadn't felt quite the same. Samuel, in particular, had been affected by it deeply (or so Jupiter was later told). Just nineteen then and not yet in charge, he had paced around the house for an entire week after Jupiter's birth with a distant gaze in his eyes, snapping violently at anyone who dared speak to him. But he had never quite figured out where these worrisome feelings came from, not then or in all the years after. Or why, no matter how hard he tried to crush it, the spirit and optimism of his slaves had burned like an unquenchable fire from the day that Jupiter arrived.

His mere presence there was a balm to their wounds. The words of encouragement he spoke to them each night after the day's trials were heard for exactly what they were: the soothings of an angel sent just for them.

For twenty-six years he had served this mission. He had loved these people like brothers and sisters, mothers and fathers. And so, having to tell them all last night that he was leaving them on the morrow had been more challenging than any beating he'd ever endured.

Jupiter had resisted the command at first, determined to see his mission through. But the things revealed to him in his dreams were indisputable; if he didn't leave soon, Samuel was going to kill him.

The man might not have been half as smart as he thought he was, but his instincts were indeed sharp. Though he had never come close to figuring out what it was, he had sensed that something was off about Jupiter right from the beginning. His distrust had grown more and more, it seemed, as time went on. Recently, it had begun to reach dangerous levels.

"What art thou?" Samuel had asked him a week ago today, with the sun not yet risen and the rest of the plantation asleep. His voice was cold and forceful as always, but there was an undertone of bewilderment, too.

"Thy slave," Jupiter replied. The words were difficult to get out through the pain. His arms had been stretched by a rope that looped over the east barn's rafters. His back was bruised and bleeding from so many whiplashes he'd lost count.

"No. Thou art something else." A few more lashes and Samuel had grown bored. Or perhaps divine intervention had diverted his attention, for it was that night in the frantic dreams of shallow, anguished sleep that Jupiter had received his first warning to leave.

Though the command tore at his heart, his place was to obey. He'd only been waiting for the right opportunity ever since.

Then, at last, the heavens broke, and the rain began to fall. He had sensed it coming (been told it was coming?) yesterday, even while the skies were still bright and clear. Now, as the first drops splashed against his dust-coated skin, Jupiter felt a wave of bittersweet emotions wash over him at the same time.

He waited a couple minutes longer, until the clouds had fully ruptured and their water came down in torrents.

"Keep working!" the overseer named Edward Smith shouted. "'Tis but a bit of rain!"

Jupiter lifted his eyes just enough to watch the man walk past him between the tobacco rows. He waited until Edward was ten, maybe fifteen paces away, until the blue-gray material of his coat became a blur and he disappeared into the deluge.

Then Jupiter sprang up and took off running. Dirt that was quickly turning to mud squelched beneath his bare feet. The wind and rain drove against his face and made it impossible to see where he was going, but he knew the way. Just a half a mile across the field in the north direction and he'd reach the forest. If he could make it there, he could lose them.

Jupiter picked up his speed. The ground at his feet was all that he could see, and it flew by in a blur. He felt a surge of determination lift his spirit, and a laugh almost escaped his lips.

Then a tall figure stepped in front of him.

Unable to stop in time, Jupiter slammed into it, taking the brunt of the impact himself and falling to the ground while the figure just stumbled back a step and craned its head to see what struck it. Through the haze of rain, Jupiter saw Samuel staring down at him. He looked confused at first and, for a brief moment, afraid. Then his eyes narrowed.

Jupiter scrambled to his feet and juked Samuel so hard the big man nearly slipped in the mud; he might not have been very strong, but Jupiter had always been quick. He felt a finger graze the collar of his shirt, then he was sprinting again.

"Runaway! Runaway!" Samuel's cries cut through the thunderstorm's roar. Jupiter didn't turn back, just pushed himself even harder. Freedom, however temporary—for he knew not where he'd be sent next—was closer than it had ever been.

He could see the forest just ahead. The shouts of Samuel and the overseers were growing more distant behind him with every bounding step. And when a musket cracked, it, too, sounded deceptively far away.

Jupiter felt a pain in his lower back like being punched. Adrenaline kept his legs churning just as fast as before, but the alarms deep within his nervous system were already starting to sound; whatever damage that angry lead ball had done, it was severe.

He crossed the edge of the forest, weaving around trees and crashing through bushes, just as the crack of a second musket firing split the air. There was a sound like that of a bee buzzing by his ear, then a small explosion of bark as the ball struck the trunk of an oak tree just a few feet from his head. Jupiter ducked even though it was a delayed reaction, then he straightened and kept running.

He only slowed when his body could go no farther. Blood streamed from the wound in his back. The tail of his shirt and left pants leg were warm and sticky with it, and he was growing dizzy from the loss. If Samuel and the overseers had pursued him at once, they probably could have followed the crimson trail themselves. But of course they'd gone for the dogs first. Those hounds were Samuel's prized possessions. And even in the pouring rain, Jupiter had no chance of losing them bleeding like he was.

He spotted a ravine just ahead and summoned the will to make it that far; his muscles were starting to weaken and tremble, his vision starting to become more of a blur than the driving rain alone could account for. By the time he made it down into the ravine and beneath an overhang of root-anchored soil, he sank to his knees and curled up into a ball on the watery ground.

Guilt pierced his soul as he lay there dying. He had abandoned his family for nothing. He had left them just to die the same as he would have if he'd stuck by their side. Had all his suffering in the world of man been just as futile? It felt that way. He didn't see how he could have ever been expected to bring light to a place so dark and wretched.

You have performed your mission well, spoke the voice inside his head. And this time, it left no doubt who was doing the speaking. Through the sheets of rain and his fading vision, he could faintly see the outline of her there with him in the ravine, glowing like a flame that burned despite the water.

And as your reward, I have three promises to make to you, my dear friend. Her familiar voice was like a blanket by the fire, stilling his shivers and spreading warmth through his body. Jupiter drew a shaky breath and let his eyelids close.

My first promise to you is that rest awaits your soul.

Jupiter let his head slump to the ground, feeling sleepy already.

My second promise is that your mortal body will never be found by those who would defile it.

The rush of rain and the wailing wind faded into silence. When she spoke again, her voice was the only sound that remained in the world he was leaving.

My third promise, dear friend, is that there will be justice for you and those whom you have loved.

He could see the light now. A pathway of brilliant radiance leading back to the home he'd left so long ago. But before he followed it, she shared with him one parting vision—a vision of a pathway entirely different from the one he was soon to follow: a road that materialized in the dense forest. And Samuel Taylor stumbling down it.

CHAPTER TEN

For a heartbeat, Jason dared to close his eyes. Just for a moment, to let his mind drift elsewhere again. Up through the misty air that sent shivers through his bare, emaciated body. Up through the veil of this surreal, nightmarish world and back to the doldrums of the world before it in which he now found sanctuary.

This time, it was the memory of drinking beers with Tyler Gentry and Ricky Meyers underneath the bridge across Little Bend River, then shooting the cans with .22s once they were empty. He could almost hear the crack of lead against aluminum just like back then before the crack of a whip and the searing pain that followed tore the illusion away.

"WORK!"

Jason set his shaking, bare foot against the step of his shovel and took another bite out of the damp earth. It was the start of the forty-third hole he'd dug in this field today. With no better way to distract himself from the pain, he'd been keeping count.

Today, it was digging holes. Yesterday, it had been moving rocks around. From dawn to dusk he'd carried stones so large he struggled to lift them from one arbitrary location in the field to another, the lash of The Slaver's whip guiding his way by correcting every stumbling, exhausted step he took in the wrong direction. The day before, he'd been made to harvest twenty bushels of the wilted, rotting tobacco that grew from the field's poisoned soil, only to watch them rot further in a putrid heap ever since.

Jason made sure the hole was at least knee-deep before he staggered out of it; that seemed to be the standard that would keep him from being kicked back down into it. Then he walked a few aimless paces and pressed his shovel into the ground again.

"Stop."

Jason froze. He gripped the cracked wood of the shovel's handle with white knuckles and stared dead-eyed into the fog. It was never good when The Slaver grew bored of watching Jason's vain labor. His methods of livening things up were always brutal. Jason focused on the sound of drunken laughter and flowing water, the smell of beer and spent gunpowder from the .22 casings.

"Art thou ready to die, Jason Baker?"

"Yes, master," he replied. It was close for him one way or another. He was dehydrated. And infected. And exhausted beyond life's limits. The promise of death lingered like a shadow in the corner of his eye, and Jason begged it night and day to stop teasing and take him.

"Speak truly, and I will let it be so." Jason heard The Slaver's boots squelching in the mud as he approached. The rotten odor of him—never far away these past two weeks—grew stronger. Jason felt the tattered hems of the thing's coat brush his skin as the monster stepped past him, and he lowered his eyes.

With the stained crotch of The Slaver's wool trousers still barely in his view, Jason watched his pale, gangly hand pull a flintlock pistol from his belt—its wood peeling and its barrel speckled with rust. He heard the screech of the corroded hammer pulling back. He felt the hollow cylinder press against the top of his head.

"*Who sent thee here?*"

I don't know wasn't the right answer. That had cost Jason his testicles the first time he was asked this question. *Benjamin Parker* wasn't it either. "*No water for lying tongues,*" The Slaver had said to this response two days ago, and Jason hadn't tasted a drop since.

"*Speak. And speak truly. Or thy death will be prolonged for days.*"

Jason closed his eyes and could hear the frogs chirping again from the banks of the Little Bend. Could feel the breeze of a hot summer night on his face.

"Jupiter," he muttered. A stab in the dark. "Jupiter sent me here."

Jason felt the flintlock's barrel press harder against his skull. "*Why?*"

"Because he's an evil son of a bitch," Jason tried; he'd never made it this far before.

The Slaver growled. "*Wrong.*" Jason felt the gun begin to lift, the swift death it promised slipping away.

"Because *I'm* evil. Because I fucking deserve it."

The Slaver stopped. He had already started to lower the gun's hammer, but Jason heard it click back into place. "*Where is he now?*"

Jason lifted his eyes and looked up the barrel, trailing up The Slaver's outstretched arm, past his wilted, rotting face, and settling on the gray sky above. If only he could rise up into it. Melt into the clouds and fall back down no longer such a tortured creature but instead a single drop of rain.

"Heaven. He's in Heaven. And this is Hell."

The Slaver trembled with sudden rage. His glazed eyes went bloodshot, as if a vessel had burst simultaneously in each one. *"DAMN THEE, JUPITER!"*

Jason saw the flash of powder igniting in the flintlock's pan a split second before blissful darkness dropped on him like a hammer.

CHAPTER ELEVEN

Benjamin forced down another bite of scrambled eggs that had gone cold minutes ago and chased it with a gulp of water. He wasn't normally one to struggle for an appetite, even with food so bland and tiresome, but the death he'd suffered at the hands of The Priestess two days ago pressed heavy on him.

He could still hear the fire crackling. He could almost feel the bronze hands of the altar growing hotter against his skin as they cradled his body above the flames.

This wasn't the first time she'd got to him, and the shtick was always the same with that bitch. But damn if it didn't still take a toll. Burning alive just never gets any easier.

When he heard the front door opening and heavy footsteps crossing its threshold, Benjamin stayed rooted at the kitchen table. Like most days on this farm tended to do, this one had just gone from miserable to more so. It was that big lug, Jason Whatshisname, no doubt. He'd been screwed up in the head before; no telling how bad it would be now after two weeks with The Slaver.

Or maybe it had done him some good. Hard to know, really, how a person would take something like that. Benjamin set his fork down and cleared his throat. "In here, son."

More footsteps. Then Jason rounded the corner into the kitchen. He pulled out the chair across from Benjamin and sat down without any acknowledgment. Looking at his eyes, Benjamin couldn't tell if he was even seeing what was around him.

"Rough couple weeks, I reckon?"

"Hmm," was Jason's only response.

"You hungry?"

"Starving."

"Yeah, I reckon that's true enough, too." Benjamin slid his half-eaten plate of eggs across the table. Jason began shoveling them into his mouth as soon as the plate stopped moving.

He choked a little when he tried to swallow and coughed a spray of crumbled yolk across the table. "Water?"

Benjamin slid his cup across, too. "There's more if you're still hungry," he said when Jason had emptied the plate. "You being gone all this time has left us with a bit of a surplus."

"Later," Jason said. A bit of his color might have returned after the food, but his eyes were still hollow and fixed on some focal point in a different space and time.

"Listen to me, son. I know it ain't easy, but the sooner you pull yourself together, the better off you're gonna be. Can't be dwelling on the last one when you've got to be getting ready for the next one, you know what I mean? Making it through The Flip without one of them things catchin' you…that's the only way this gets any more bearable."

"Is that why you ran?"

"Hell yes, it's why I ran. What'd you think I was gonna do? Come riding in to save your hide like the damn cavalry? And you shoulda run, too. They'll find you nine times out of ten if you try to hide. Especially The Slaver and them hounds of his. They might look like they've been dead a hundred years, but them noses still work good as ever."

"They didn't get you then?"

A flashback of The Priestess's bone-pierced face reflecting the firelight barged into his mind; the sound of shredded lips chanting curses while he cooked. "Not at first."

"Tell me something," Jason said after a few moments of silence.

"I'll tell you anything you want to know," Benjamin lied.

"Who is Jupiter?"

"The Roman king of the gods. If that's not the answer you're looking for, then I don't know." Benjamin forced a hint of a grin, but hearing that name made his stomach turn.

"You're lying," Jason said, his voice just as monotone despite this sudden turn in the conversation. "Jupiter is all that monster talks about. If you've spent a single day with him, then you know exactly what I'm asking you."

Benjamin felt his palms getting sweaty. He hadn't expected the big grunt to be so shrewd. "That thing's got worms where his brains used to be, son. Nonsense and gibberish is all that comes out. And Jupiter's a new one to me."

Jason shook his head. Some of the life was returning to his eyes. They no longer stared out into the distance but instead were now locked on Benjamin. "It's been a long time since you played poker, hasn't it, old man? Shit, I know you've been lying to me ever since I got here. About how much food we got. About how things actually work around here. And now this… this one's plain as day."

"You know, it takes a pretty bold man to call another a liar in his own home." Benjamin tried to sound bold himself, but his throat was tightening. If this man ever found out the truth of this place, there would be hell to pay.

"What are you going to do about it? Kill me?"

"The question ain't what I'm gonna do, son," Benjamin said. "It's what are you gonna do? See, it don't matter if you think I'm lying to you or not. It don't matter if you don't like how I treat you, or how I divvy up the food, or nothing else. There ain't a damn thing you can do about it, you see? You and me, we're stuck with each other. Ain't no amount of bloodshed gonna change that either. So you'd best forget all this nonsense and start working on making both our lives here a little less miserable."

"No," Jason said, shaking his head again. "Playing farmer here with you don't interest me anymore. I'm getting out of here."

"Oh, you are, are you? You ain't been listening, son. There is no leaving."

"So you've said."

"Don't you think I'd be gone by now if there was some way out of this place? Not sitting here trying to hide it from you for God knows what reason."

Jason shrugged. "Dunno. But I do know I'm about to get some truth out of you, old man. One way or another."

Benjamin studied him from across the table, weighing his options. It may well pale in comparison to all that he'd already endured, but he didn't doubt this man's ability to make him suffer. Overpowering Jason was a pipedream. Even making it to the rifle in the living room would only be a temporary fix, if successful.

Maybe just enough truth to cool the man's anger was what the situation called for. If he chose his words carefully, perhaps he could thread the needle between the two landmines in front of him. "Tell me what you want to know. I'll answer you truthful."

"Who's Jupiter? Let's start with that."

"Alright, alright. Maybe I do know he was. Or got an idea anyway. Not like I ever met him. Anything I know about the man is just bits and pieces I picked up while The Slaver was whipping me to death, and I'm sure you know he's not one for elaboration. But here's what I'm pretty sure about: Jupiter was The Slaver's *someone special*."

"Someone special?"

"Yeah, someone special, alright. *Really special*. Someone he made a big mistake killing."

"So what, he got sent here? Like a punishment?"

"That's about the sum of it." Benjamin watched him. He didn't know if Jason believed it, but so far he'd told him the truth.

"And the rest of them?"

"The Avengers you mean?"

"I'm not calling them that," Jason said. "Fucking stupid name."

"Yeah, they all killed someone special, too. That's why they're all here."

"So they're human?"

"They used to be."

"What about us then?"

"What about us?" Benjamin asked, dreading where the conversation was headed.

"Why are we here?"

Benjamin stared at him for a moment, wondering if he'd figure it out himself. "Same reason they are, son. Hell, I can tell you already know it. Who was she? I'm guessing it was a woman for you. You probably felt it the moment you saw her, too, didn't you? And tell me if I'm wrong, but when she died, was it the closest thing your withered soul has ever felt to guilt? I'm sure you didn't understand it, but I bet you still felt it. The sheer *magnitude* of what you'd just done."

Jason still looked blank and unreadable. But his gaze was distant again now, and all the fire in it was gone. "If that's true, why aren't we like them?"

This was the question Benjamin had been waiting for. Dreading. If this born killer found out now, after what he'd just endured, that being on the other side of the torment was an option, he'd take that deal in a blink. Probably without even trying to understand the consequences. Benjamin focused on keeping his voice smooth and steady and delivered his prepared response.

"They weren't always like that either. They showed up here just like me and you." That much was true. For the most part.

"What happened."

And now, the all-important lie. "Something changed 'em. No rhyme or reason to it. It's happened to every one of 'em so far, except us. I reckon it'll come around for us eventually, too, just no telling when. Your old buddy The Scarecrow used to be a little mute brat named Leon Kingsley. He was only here two weeks before he turned. Some of the others took a few years. And hell, I done lost count how many years I been here without turning yet."

Without *choosing to* yet, like all the rest had done. Most of them had made their choice without a second thought, just like this troglodyte surely would as well if he ever found out he had the option.

But Jason latched on to some other detail instead, skipping right over the part that mattered. "So you were the first one here?"

"That's right," Benjamin said, relieved that the truth was safe to tell again for now.

"But The Slaver..."

"Born in 1722, so he said. Makes him about 200 years my elder. Almost 300 years yours. But he was the third one to get here, after myself and the mute boy."

"How's that possible?"

Benjamin snorted. "Hell, how's any of it possible, son? Everything that's happened so far and a little time travel's what's got you in a twist? I got a theory, though, see, that it ain't even time travel at all. I don't think this farm exists in the same... what's the damn word... the same *dimension* as the one we came from. Outside of space and time, you understand? That's how come people can be from all different places and all different times and still wander down that same road and end up here."

He could see Jason growing bored with this theorizing, but that was good; the quicker he lost interest in the topic of how men became monsters the better.

"Why wouldn't you just tell me all this before?"

"Listen to me," Benjamin said. He was growing more comfortable now. Had the big sap right where he wanted him. "Your sanity is all you got to hold onto here. Now, you never know how someone's gonna react when you tell 'em that the only light at the end of this awful tunnel is that they eventually get to become the very thing that's been tormenting 'em. In my experience, the realities of this place are something that it's best to ease a person into. Not something you dump on 'em all at once as soon as they get here."

You just think I forgot how to lie, you milk-mouthed whippersnapper, Benjamin thought with a twinge of pride.

"Well, if it makes you feel any better, old man," Jason said, "after two weeks with Yankee Doodle Zombie, I'd a whole lot rather be one of them anyway. I'd *welcome it*."

I bet you would.

"I wouldn't be so sure. Did that thing look like a happy, fulfilled man to you, son? Don't matter none either way, though. Your time'll come when it comes."

"We'll see about that. None of this changes what I said. I'm finding a way out of here." Jason leaned forward then and fixed him in a simmering glare. "And that starts with you being an open book from now on, you understand, old man? No more sparing my feelings bullshit. I want to know everything you know. Because here's the deal: if I even get the suspicion you're hiding something from me, I'm going to split you from asshole to Adam's apple and wait for you to come back so we can try again."

Benjamin sighed. "I'd tell you that violence isn't going to solve anything. *Again*. But I get the feeling it's like telling a fish not to piss in the ocean."

"I mean it, old man. I've got nothing left to lose."

Benjamin watched him in the dying light of sunset that seeped through the kitchen window. There wasn't a scratch on him anymore that hadn't healed, but his time with The Slaver had still changed even his physical appearance. He had eyes like a wolf before. Now he had eyes like a caged one.

"I'll tell you whatever you want to know. But, right now, best way I can help you is if you told me more about yourself first."

"How's that going to help me?"

"You want to figure out how to get out? Might as well start with figuring out how you got here in the first place."

"What do you mean?"

"I seen the way you looked when I talked about your someone special. You already know who she is. And I promise you she's the reason you're here. So tell me about her. Then maybe I can tell you a bit about her myself."

Jason fell silent. His eyes twitched a little at the corners. For a long while, Benjamin couldn't tell if he was about to break down sobbing or jump up swinging. When he finally spoke, his voice was distant. Almost disembodied, as if it were translating now for a mind that had picked up and gone somewhere else. "Her name was Amanda Williams."

Amanda's Mission

There are times when a person's entire destiny boils down to just a single action. Today, June 7th, 2024, Amanda Williams was about to realize hers.

There'd been tennis practices and birthday parties as a kid; high school, then community college, then a job waiting tables at Shogun's Japanese Steakhouse after that—an entire lifetime she'd lived dutifully, knowing all the while that it was building to this day.

She checked the clock on the dash of her Kia Soul and did some quick math in her head. It was 7:46 p.m. now, which meant the bus would arrive in exactly forty-three minutes—a long time to wait stranded on the side of the highway, but when you've spent your entire life preparing for one single tick of the clock's minute hand, it's a lot better to be early than late.

She rolled down the car windows and let in the forest air. A wren trilled from somewhere in the pines. Even closer, a woodpecker thrummed its beak against a hollow trunk. This stretch of Highway 278 was just as scenic as described, winding through the foothills of the Appalachians in northern Alabama. But the same things that made the drive pleasant—the drop-offs, the switchback turns, the trees that grew so close to the road they served as its only guardrails—made it dangerous, too.

Ted McGillicuddy (the driver of the bus she was waiting on) wasn't taking this route for the scenery, though. The road might have demanded caution, but it was still the fastest route from Longbow High School to Tucker Ridge High School. The Tucker Ridge Wildcats had defeated the Longbow Golden Arrows seven to five in the first round of the state baseball tournament according to the radio. Now, the team was ready to get home and celebrate, and Ted was ready to get home and go to bed.

When she closed her eyes, it was like she could see through his. He was just switching on the bus's headlights as the day's sunlight began to fade. His eyelids were heavy, but he would never fall asleep on the job. Twenty-eight years he'd driven a bus for Tucker Ridge High. There was not a single thing in his life he took more seriously than the safety of his "youngins", as he'd taken to calling them around the time he grew old enough to be their grandfather. Today, unfortunately, the calamity waiting a little farther down the road was one entirely out of his control.

Well, he could have eaten a little better and exercised more, Amanda supposed, but she wasn't going to fault him too much for that. No one can predict a heart attack, especially at his age. No one except those who'd sent her to intervene.

Closing her eyes again, she could see a different scene. A vision of what was soon to come if she wasn't there to stop it. She saw Ted lurch forward into the steering wheel, his jaw clenched tight as the sudden agony ripped through his chest. She saw his chin droop as his vision faded black, then she saw the front of the bus steadily veering off the highway, crossing first the rumble strip on the shoulder with a gyrating buzz, then tilting sharply downward as it began its plummet down the mountainside.

The rest was branded on her mind just as clearly—the ruined bodies and anguished cries; the smoke and the blood and the crumpled steel. Dark as it was, this vision had been her most common daydream. Knowing she was going to stop it from happening made it much more motivating than depressing.

She checked the clock again—7:59—then she checked her purse to make sure once more that the bottle of Aspirin was tucked safe inside. She took a deep breath of the forest-scented air to steady her nerves.

At 8:29 on the dot, Ted McGillicutty and the Wildcats baseball team would pull up to where she was stopped on the narrow shoulder. Unlike the ticking of a heart, the mind of man could not be so easily predicted. And yet, knowing Ted and the kind of man he was, there was no doubt that he would stop to help a young woman stranded on a barren highway with darkness fast approaching. That she was pretty and blonde might have been a motivating factor for some men, but not Ted. No one in his small community knew, but he'd never been very interested in pretty women. When he stopped, it would be out of the goodness of his heart.

And when that heart failed four minutes later, he'd be safe on the shoulder helping her instead of behind the wheel. She'd be there to administer aid, and all the children on the bus would be saved, too. Some would probably go on to call her their guardian angel. Even the ones who swore by this would never really know just how right they were.

And then...then it would soon be time to go back home. Amanda couldn't feel the cancer in her body yet, but she knew that it was there. Unlike those born rather than sent, she had always known the path her life would take—and where it would end. She didn't fear it. Not in the slightest. But she did mourn for those she'd be leaving behind almost as much as she longed for reunion with those she'd left.

Another check of the clock on the dash. 8:04 now. Outside her Kia, the shadows the trees cast on the highway were starting to meld into the surrounding darkness as the last gasps of twilight trickled through the woods. Amanda flipped on her headlights and hazards and took a long, deep breath.

There were still a few birds singing from the trees, but most had begun to go silent. Now, the wind moving the leaves and branches was all she heard through the car's open windows. Then, somewhere in the distance farther down the road, the rumble of an engine.

It grew steadily louder as it climbed the hill, approaching from the opposite direction the bus was supposed to come from. Amanda bit the bottom of her lip and hastily flipped her hazards and headlights back off again. Whoever it was, she had to hope they didn't stop. If they were still there when Ted drove by, he probably wouldn't see any reason to stop himself. She needed to think up something to send them on their way—and quick—just in case they turned out to be the good Samaritan type.

The engine growled as the approaching vehicle reached a

particularly steep incline, and Amanda saw headlights spilling across the turn just ahead.

Please don't stop, she prayed. *Just this once, don't try to be helpful.*

The pickup truck—she could see that's what it was now, a rusted white work truck with ladder racks on the bed—wasn't going very fast when it rounded the turn. But when its headlights lit up her windshield and caused Amanda to squint, the truck slowed to a crawl.

No....

The truck crossed the centerline and pulled over on the shoulder in front of her. She heard gravel crunch beneath its thick treads, then the squeak of its brakes as it came to a stop. Its front bumper was just a few feet in front of hers, the driver probably assuming she might need a jumpstart, and its headlights were still blaring through her windshield. They went off, and the truck's door opened.

A man stepped out. In the darkness, Amanda couldn't see exactly what he looked like, but she could tell by his size that he was most definitely a man. Her heart sped up a little faster.

"Dead battery?" the man said.

"No, I...um—"

"'Cause I can give you a jump, if you want. I got cables in my toolbox." He bent over a little so that she could see his face through the driver's side window. He had stonework features and a mess of dark brown hair. A breeze moved through the car, carrying with it his scent of motor oil and sweat.

"No. Thank you. That's not the problem, I don't think. There's actually a tow truck on the way already. Should be here any minute. But I really appreciate you offering to help. Truly."

"You know getting a tow all the way out here is gonna cost you, right? A couple hundred bucks at least. Let me take a look at it. I'm pretty handy with this sort of thing."

"Really, that isn't necessary. I don't want to inconvenience you, and—"

"Wouldn't be no trouble at all, ma'am. I ain't in no rush." He circled around to the front of the car and started running his fingers underneath the hood in search of the release latch. "Pop the hood for me, would you?"

Amanda's eyes darted to the clock. It was 8:14. Just fifteen minutes before the bus would be passing by. No more time left for being pleasant—she had to get him out of here now.

"Sir, I'm just going to wait for the tow truck."

"Well hell, I mean, I'm here already. I might as well—"

"No, that's alright. I don't mean to be rude, but I'd be more comfortable waiting for the tow truck. So please, it was kind of you to stop, but I would prefer it if you got back in your truck and had a wonderful rest of the night."

She could faintly see the moonlight glow in his eyes as he stared at her for seconds that dragged on. "Shit, lady, whatever you say. Try to do something nice for a person."

He turned around and took a step back toward the still-open door of his truck. Amanda silently exhaled.

Then she breathed in sharply and held it in again when she saw him top and turn back around.

"You know, it's women like you's what's wrong with the world," he said, pointing his finger at her through the windshield as he walked back toward her car. "Running around, treating every guy they meet like he's some kind of creep."

Amanda felt for the window switch on the door, cringing at the thought of how long it would take to roll up. "Please, I don't want—"

"Don't you touch that fucking switch." The man's voice had dropped an octave. His arm reached into the cab so quickly it was a blur. Beneath Amanda's chin, a knife appeared from nowhere. She could feel its edge already biting at her throat—a pinprick of pain and a pen drop of blood.

"Unbuckle your seatbelt."

"You don't understand what you're doing," Amanda pleaded. The vision of the school bus careening off the mountainside was all she could think about.

"Right now, lady. Nice and slow, but right now."

Amanda moved her hand away from the window switch and pressed the belt's latch. It retracted with a high-pitched whine.

"Open the door."

"Listen to me..." Amanda started, but her words died on a lurch of breath when she felt the knife press into her windpipe a dangerous bit harder.

"Lady, I will saw your head off right here on the side of the road if you make me. Now open the goddamn door."

Amanda hesitated for a moment, then she pulled the handle. The final barrier between her and this psychopath cracked open.

The hand not holding the knife pulled it open the rest of the way, then grabbed her roughly by the hair. "Out."

Amanda stepped out onto the asphalt. Her head was craned

awkwardly by the way the man held her, and he kept the knife pressed firmly against her throat.

"Walk," he said, turning her toward his truck. "And keep your mouth shut."

Amanda obeyed the first command, but not the second. "Just listen to me. Please. There's a school bus coming. If I'm not here to stop it, a lot of kids are going to die."

"Shut up and get in." He moved the knife away from her throat just long enough to open the truck's passenger door.

Amanda stood and stared for a moment through the open door, saw dirt and beer cans on the floorboards, stains on the truck's beige seats. It felt like looking into a coffin. *Her* coffin.

Whether she got in or not, she was probably going to die. But at least if she made him kill her here, there was a chance the scene might still cause Ted to stop the bus. If she let this man drive away with her now and left only an abandoned car on the side of the road, it was doubtful he'd even slow down.

Amanda made up her mind. She drew what she realized might be her final breath, then she twisted and drove her fist into the man's crotch. He grunted and flinched, losing his grip on her hair when he doubled over. The instant she was free, Amanda took off running.

She sprinted down the middle of the highway, wishing now she'd chosen track all those years ago instead of tennis. The man was yelling at her from not too far behind, and she could already hear the rhythmic thud-thud-thud of his terribly long strides.

If she could just evade him long enough, she could force the bus to stop. Five, maybe ten minutes of running was all it would take before she met it. Amanda pushed her body harder than she ever had.

But it wasn't enough. Not even close.

It felt like her weight suddenly tripled as her pursuer wrapped her in a tackle, and her legs buckled instantly. She landed hard on her knees and elbows, then quickly flattened all the way underneath his mass. Amanda lifted her head and tried to push herself up, but the giant sandwiching her against the asphalt didn't budge.

"You're going to regret that," he growled. Then he wrapped the crook of his arm around her neck and started to squeeze. Amanda felt her head begin to swim. As her consciousness slipped away, she had only one aching regret.

Seven minutes later, a Tucker Ridge High School bus crossed that spot on the road where she'd passed out. Not one of the raucous boys on board noticed the few droplets of angel blood on the pavement. The driver, Ted McGillicuddy, did notice the old Kia Soul on the side of the road and slowed down a little. But, seeing it empty, he pressed the bus's accelerator again.

He took a deep breath when the abandoned car was well behind them, eager for home and supper and his bed. Then he flinched at a sudden, sharp pain in his chest.

Jason's Transgression

Jason Baker glared at the television a few seconds longer, then turned off the set. The bus wreck up on 278 was the talk of the news. Even the national networks were covering the story. Eleven of the bus's seventeen passengers, including the driver, were pronounced dead on the scene. Three of the six survivors had to be airlifted to Huntsville Hospital.

He tried again to remember exactly what that bitch had said about a bus. Something about stopping it and people dying. The whole thing didn't settle well with him. It wasn't the part about those kids dying that bothered him; kids died somewhere in the world every minute. But the timing and location of the wreck and whatever it was she'd said about it beforehand—that part put a knot in his stomach.

The lingering dread he just couldn't shake had spoiled his first night with his new toy. He had locked her in the storm cellar after arriving home at his single-wide trailer deep in the woods south of Cullman, Alabama, and he hadn't paid her a visit since.

Most of his toys would have already served their purpose and met their end by now, but the thought of seeing her again filled him with strange fear.

It was pissing him off more than anything. She was the one who should have been afraid. While the storm cellar and walls of his trailer muffled all but the loudest screams, every woman he'd locked down there so far had been more than equal to the task. Not this one, though; Jason hadn't heard a peep out of her.

He pulled another brown bottle from the six-pack next to his musty recliner and twisted off the cap. What he needed to do was get good and drunk. Then he'd feel like paying her a visit.

Four beers later, it happened just like he predicted. His courage returned. And his libido, too. Even with no makeup and a bloody nose (actually, who was he kidding? The bloody nose was a plus), she sure had been a pretty little thing. He'd been struck by her the moment he saw her sitting in her car and had decided right away that she would be his next.

Seemed kind of fitting that he'd have such a special one as his seventh. That had always been Jason's favorite number. Special or not, he'd do her just like all the rest: his seven inches first, then the Bowie knife's after that.

The thought brought a stirring to his loins, and Jason stood up, his body warm and buzzing from the alcohol. He swiped the keychain off the hook on the trailer's thin wall and headed out the door.

The night air was still and muggy. Frogs chirped from the tall grass near the woods at the edge of his unkempt lawn, and he saw a cottontail rabbit bound across his dirt driveway. Lucky little bastard that he didn't have his .22 on him. Cottontails were good eating.

The storm cellar was just on the other side of the trailer, its steel door only a thin concrete base from being flush with the ground. It had cost him a couple grand to put it in three years ago, back when he was making decent money working as a welder. An expensive bit of paranoia, some had said, but they didn't know its real purpose.

In no real rush (was he savoring the moment or dreading it? Maddeningly, he still wasn't sure), Jason made his way over to the cellar. He bent down and fumbled with the padlock on the door, struggling to get the key in the hole. Better luck with that in a minute, he hoped; he liked to give his girls a good showing before they left this world.

The key turned, and the lock sprang open. Jason put it and the keys in his pocket, then he slung open the cellar door with one hard jerk, sending it screaming across its metal track and clanging against the doorstop.

At the bottom of the concrete staircase, the woman stared up at him, her face aglow in LED light from the battery-powered lantern he kept down here whenever there were guests. If she'd even flinched at this violent entrance, he'd missed it. She sure didn't seem very frightened. Jason felt the knot in his stomach twist tighter.

"They're dead," she said. "Eleven already, and two more will die before the night's over. All because of you."

It took Jason a beat to realize what she was talking about.

"How do you know that?" he asked. He had taken her phone from her and ditched it out the window at the first bridge they crossed, and if she had another that he'd missed, then the entire Cullman County Sheriff's Department would have been here already. There was no way she could have found out about the bus wreck. Of course, there's no way she could have known about before it ever happened either, but she'd seemed to from what he could remember. "Tell me how you know about the bus."

Amanda shook her head. "I'm not talking to you anymore."

Normally, that would've suited Jason just fine; he'd never been one for pillow talk. But some deep-down voice screaming in the wells of his black soul urged him to wait. This woman huddled on the dirt floor of his cramped cellar looked like a work of priceless art before him, even in these destitute conditions. She had an aura about her that filled the room and filled him with wonder and fear.

"Talk to me, and I won't kill you." It was a lie, an obvious one to any rational person, but the kind he'd found most people were willing to believe when they had no other hope.

"Honestly, I'd rather you just get it over with."

Jason was taken aback. It took him a moment to find his next words. "Alright…talk to me and I won't do it slowly."

This seemed to get a bit more of a reaction, though even it was subtle. "I don't care what you do to me, Jason," she said once she'd gathered her nerve again. "You've got a few months before cancer is going to finish the job for you. Nothing you can possibly do between now and then is going to be worse than what you've already done."

Jason didn't know what she meant, because the only wear on her right now was a skinned knee and a busted-up nose. And that was vanilla foreplay compared to the depths he could take her to. But then something else she'd said registered and confused him even more. "Hey!...hey, how'd you know my name?"

"I know everything about you, Jason," the woman said, still staring vacantly into his eyes. "I know you were in the foster system until you turned eighteen. I know that the abuse you suffered during that time was horrendous, and that it wasn't your fault. But what you've done with that pain since then definitely is."

Jason's ears began to ring, and he touched his temples as if it would make the feeling go away. What she'd just said was true. Or it had been, in some other lifetime. One he'd done everything he could to forget—and succeeded, by and large.

"What are you?" he asked, his head bobbing on waves of alcohol and bewilderment. "Some kind of stalker?"

The woman laughed, then coughed a little and spat a spray of bloody saliva onto the dirt floor. "That's funny. From you."

"No one knows about that. No one, you hear me? So how the fuck do you?"

"I could tell you the truth," she said after some consideration. "But you wouldn't believe me if I did."

"Try me. Before I lose my patience."

She stared at him. Jason could only look at her intensely bright eyes for a moment before he had to look away. "I'm an angel,

Jason," she said eventually. "I was sent from Heaven to stop that school bus from crashing. And you prevented that."

"You're crazy is what you are."

"Like I said. I should've known better than to cast pearls before swine."

Jason shook his head, unable to make any sense of what she was saying yet pierced by the words in a way he also couldn't understand. "You should've known better than to stop in the middle of nowhere at night. What the hell were you doing out there anyway? You didn't...it didn't have to end up like this."

The woman gave no answer. She just leaned her head back against the cinderblock wall and closed her eyes. Almost like she was about to fall asleep. Which she was, in a sense, but Jason didn't like how she embraced it so calmly.

He wasn't liking any of this. These moments in the cellar had always been the most rapturous of his life, and this one most of all was supposed to be special—his seventh kill and a woman so exquisitely beautiful it defied all reason. And yet all he felt was unease; a low whine in his ears and a current running through his nerves that had him as jittery as a rabbit.

He wasn't in the mood for sex anymore, even though the Korean girl he'd brought down here six months ago had been his last time with a woman. The woman huddled in front of him now was more perfect and radiant than anything he'd ever had the pleasure of destroying. And yet, more than anything, he just wanted her gone.

The only question was what to do with her. That had never been a question with any of the others who ended up in his cellar. They had always come out of the cellar in trash bags. But for some bewildering reason, the thought of killing this one made his head spin.

"What's your name?" he asked.

"Which one?" Jason just stared at her, not sure what to say. "Amanda Williams. That's the one I was born with. I doubt you could pronounce the other one anyway."

"Where are you from?"

A soft smile touched her bruised lips, but she kept her head back and her eyes closed. "You keep asking questions with two different answers...Birmingham is where I was born. I've already told you where I came from."

Jason rubbed his eyelids with calloused fingers. He wanted this to be over. In a way, it reminded him of his first kill, back before he'd built up his confidence and his anxiety was through the roof. In other ways, being in the presence of this woman reminded him of nothing he'd ever experienced before.

"I think we're about done talking, Amanda."

She took a long breath, then slowly opened her eyes. "I know that nothing is going to stop you from doing what you're about to do. But it still won't be too late for you even once it's over. I want you to remember that. It's never too late to repent."

Jason unclasped the buckle on the leather sheath clipped to his belt and slid the Bowie knife from it. Its polished blade caught a glint of the lantern light and reflected it onto the woman's face like the glow of a halo.

"I don't have any choice," he said, speaking to himself as much as her. "You've seen my face. You know my name. Where I live."

"You always have a choice, Jason."

He bent down to where she was seated and moved a strand of honey-colored hair away from her neck. The brush of her skin against his fingers felt electrifying—not in a sensual way, but like actually touching a bolt of lightning. It had caught him so off guard when he tackled her on the highway that he almost recoiled and rolled off her. It felt even stronger now in this enclosed space where the trapped air seemed to hum with her energy.

"I won't make you suffer. You're too special to suffer."

"Thank you," the woman said, surprising him yet again and staying his hand a little longer.

He studied her one last time. Swam for a few more moments more in the crystal pools of her eyes. Soaked in the sun-like glow of her skin. Then, true to his word, he ended her life in an instant. In one sweeping, practiced slash of his blade. Except this time, there'd been no thrill in it. It had been more like jumping off the high dive or pulling a tooth—something he had to clear his thoughts and get over with before he could change his mind.

The woman slumped, a waterfall of blood cascading down her breasts and stomach. Jason felt a rush like all the oxygen leaving the room. The lantern sitting on the floor flickered out, then seemed to come back dimmer than before. A weight like a lead anchor dropped in his chest and settled in his bowels, dragging him down to his knees.

He could hear voices somewhere distant. Somewhere close. All around. They screamed and prayed and wept while the earth beneath his hands and knees trembled at the sound. The last thing Jason could remember was weeping along with them.

Daylight flooding through the cellar door and the sound of someone having a fit slowly brought Jason awake.

"Jason? Oh...oh my god. Jason! What in the world, man?"

Jason rolled over and opened his eyes, shielding them with a bloodstained hand when the rectangle of light coming through the open door proved too intense. Someone was standing at the top of the stairs, a tall, lanky silhouette with a fishing pole in one hand and a tackle box in the other—at least before these slipped from his grip and clattered down the steps.

"Ricky, just wait."

Ricky did not wait. He spun on his heels and sprinted away before Jason could get up, leaving the tackle box and fishing pole behind in a cloud of dust. Jason heard the sputter of a dirt bike's motor kickstart to life, then the spray of gravel from its tires as it tore down his drive and faded away down the road.

Jason glanced at the ashen body on the floor, his head buzzing as it dawned on him just all that the boy had seen. Ricky Meyers had always treated Jason like an older brother. But he had an actual older brother, too, named Kyle who he lived with in a cabin about a mile down the highway, and Kyle didn't think much of Jason at all. Ricky would tell his brother what he'd seen first, then Kyle would be the one to call the cops. Jason could see it all playing out in his head as clear as a movie.

He didn't have much time. It wouldn't take long for this little game of telephone to play out. Then, once the boys in blue got out here and had a look for themselves, there'd be dogs and road-blocks and probably even a chopper in the skies.

With no other choice, Jason decided to run. Yet it occurred to him as he stuffed as much food as he could fit in his back-pack that he would have run even if Ricky hadn't found him. Something hung in the air here now and probably always would even after that body in his cellar was removed. The weight of what he'd done was crushing, even if he didn't understand why. It, as much as the sirens soon to be screaming down his road, was the reason why he ran.

CHAPTER TWELVE

Turning a crank that lowered a metal pail down into the well, Jason felt like a character in an old Western movie. For a moment, anyway. Until the bars of this place pressed in on him again and it became difficult to breathe. He leaned against the stone wellhead and tried to keep from puking into their drinking water.

Some twenty or thirty feet down, he could barely make out his reflection on the glassy surface, a featureless silhouette staring back at him. Jason gave the crank a few more turns until the pail hit the water and turned the reflection into a shimmer of ripples. It gave him an odd feeling looking down that well. Made him eager to be away from it as soon as he retrieved the pail.

"Set it down on the counter there and start peeling those potatoes," Benjamin said when he returned with the water. Jason set the pail next to the cast iron sink where Benjamin was trimming the fat off a chicken.

Things had been more cordial with the old man in the two days since Jason escaped The Slaver (if you could call a lead ball to the brainpan escape). Benjamin had been more generous with the food since then. More generous with the truth, too, though it was still hard to tell what he didn't know from what he was hiding.

Benjamin claimed to not know a lot. He didn't know what the farm was, or how to leave it. He didn't know what caused The Flip, or what turned the people who end up here into monsters. But he was sure about one thing: this farm was the penalty for murder. The murder of *someone special.* Jason could never get a clear answer from him what that meant—another detail he claimed not to know. But it still rang true. Amanda Williams had been special. According to Benjamin, they'd all hurt someone special.

"I got another question," Jason said as he slid the blade of his knife across a russet potato. The rest was left inferred: *answer it truthfully or it'll be your skin getting peeled off next.*

"You know, son, it'd be nice if you could get all these questions of yours out at once. That way I don't have to keep playing schoolteacher all the time."

"Things come to me slowly."

Benjamin chuckled. "Yeah, I reckon they do. Go on then. What's your question?"

"The Slaver took me somewhere. Someplace I hadn't seen before."

"Took you to his hidey-hole is what he did."

"Huh?"

"That's what I call 'em anyway. They're like...little pockets of this place. No way to get to 'em until The Flip happens. Not that you'd want to anyhow."

"What are they?"

"I just told you," Benjamin said, sounding exasperated. "I still don't think you're quite able to wrap your noggin around the situation, son." He stopped what he was doing and gave Jason his full attention. "Like I said before, space and time don't work the same here. When The Flip happens, you can step through a door or into a ditch or down a...well, anyway, there's a lot of 'em around here, and they all take you someplace else. 'Course most the time you're being dragged through it, not stepping into it yourself. But if one of them decides to take you back to their hidey-hole, then you're in for a hurtin'. Whole lot easier when they just kill you on the spot."

"Like The Scarecrow did."

"Yeah, that one don't play around much. Not usually. He's got a hidey-hole, too, though. I've seen it before. Perfect replica of Willow Heights High School. Far as I know anyway. Not like I ever seen the real place. Got some kind of fancy-looking rifle he keeps in there, too, and he'll shoot you graveyard dead with it. I reckon he'll get around to taking you there eventually, if you have enough run-ins with him. But it's still a quick way to go, I suppose. All that to say, if you're gonna let one of 'em catch you, The Scarecrow's the one to pick."

"Which one's the worst?" Jason asked.

Benjamin rubbed his whiskers. "Just depends. The Slaver's a pretty bad one. But if you hate burning alive as much as I do, then The Priestess is the worst. Or if getting bent over and used like a woman before you die sounds worse, then it's The Ice

Cream Man. I'll tell you what, though, bad as all the others are, it's The Scientist that gives me the shivers. Something just ain't right about that one."

"So all of them then. All of them except The Scarecrow."

Benjamin sighed. "Yeah, that's about the sum of it. Except make no mistake, ole Leon can be a mean son of a bitch, too. He don't always aim for the heart with that damn fork of his."

"I'm going to find a way out of here," Jason said. "As soon as I have a plan."

"Well, whenever you come up with one, son, you let me know."

Jason looked up from his half-peeled potato and watched the old man for a moment, but Benjamin didn't notice. He was too busy transferring the pail of water Jason had fetched into a pot on the wood stove.

Jason still didn't trust him. He had a feeling the old man was hiding something from him. Whatever it was, all he had to do was keep him talking, and he'd figure it out eventually.

"I just realized something," Jason said.

"What's that?"

"You never told me her name."

"Whose name?" Benjamin asked. But Jason could tell he knew who.

"Your someone special. You never told me much of anything about her, come to think of it."

"I told you everything that matters, son."

"How about you just tell me everything," Jason said, fixing him in a stare. "I'll decide for myself what matters."

Benjamin looked straight ahead. His gray-blue eyes had suddenly turned into a stormy sea, deep and glistening and a maelstrom of emotion. "I'm...I'm not going to talk about her."

"That so, old man?" Jason gripped the peeling knife tight in his hand. A smile touched his lips when he caught Benjamin looking at it. "I think you ought to reconsider."

When Jason saw the sorrow in Benjamin's eyes harden into defiance, it took him by surprise. "You do whatever you're gonna do, son. Sick and tired of all your underhanded threats anyhow. I told you she was perfect. I told you what I did to her and what the cost was, and that's all you need to know. Not because I'm hiding something from you...but because it's none of your goddamn business. So either you get to cutting or hand me those taters so I can finish cooking our dinner."

Jason weighed the two options carefully. He'd never seen the old man get so emotional. It piqued his interest, but it also signaled that Benjamin was probably telling the truth; whatever history he was hiding, it was only because it was deeply personal. And painful. Carving it out of him was tempting nevertheless, but when his stomach growled, Jason handed over the potatoes.

He watched Benjamin dump them and the chicken into the pot and daydreamed of the food he used to enjoy: bacon cheeseburgers and bean burritos and fries dipped in buffalo sauce.

"What's your favorite restaurant, old man?" Jason asked once he figured Benjamin had enough time to cool down.

"What kind of question is that?" Benjamin asked as he stirred the pot of soup.

"Dunno. You want to go back to the other one?"

"Howard Johnson's" Benjamin grumbled after a short pause.

"Never heard of it."

"They used to be everywhere."

"Just how old are you anyway?"

"Not sure. Keeping track of time got hard after a while. But I was born in 1923. And it was 1956 when I showed up here."

"That'd make you one hundred and one years old."

"Do I look a hundred years old to you, son?" Benjamin asked, staring at him like he was an idiot. Then, a little under his breath—but not so much that Jason couldn't hear it: "God almighty, it's like talking to a fencepost."

"What's that, old man?"

"Listen," Benjamin said. "I'm gonna try and go over this one more time. I reckon I been on this farm about thirty, forty years or so. Now, I know that don't make much sense to you, because I just said I got here in '56 and that was what...seventy years ago as far as you're concerned? But as far as The Slaver's concerned, it's about two hundred years in the future. I don't even know how many thousands of years in the future The Priestess would tell you 1956 is, if she could speak a lick of English that is. And if you asked The Scientist, he'd tell you it was over a century in the past. Except that one would be smart enough to understand to what's actually going on here."

"Which one's right?"

Benjamin set his stirring spoon down and threw up his hands. "You're still not gettin' it! Ain't none of 'em right! Ain't none of 'em wrong neither. It's all *relative,* son."

Jason blinked at him. Benjamin just sighed and shook his head.

"You've aged, though, right?" Jason said. "Since you've been here."

"That's right. I was a young man when I got here. Once I realized how things work, how every scrape and scratch on you heals when you get brought back, I wondered if aging stopped, too. Didn't work that way, though. As you can see."

"So what happens when..." Jason trailed off, not sure how to articulate what he was wondering.

"When it gets to the point that even if I'm resurrected, I'm so old and shriveled up I just die of old age again as soon as it happens? I don't know. But that's what I aim to find out."

Jason thought about this for a minute. "So that's your plan, then? You're just gonna wait until you're a corpse and hope it ends there?"

"Yeah, that's the plan. Far as I've got one anyway. Now ask yourself this, son, 'cause I can still see that wild gleam in your eye, like you're about to head for the hills any second: if there was any way out of this place besides that, don't you think I'd have tried it by now?"

"Doesn't matter," Jason said. "Just because you haven't found a way doesn't mean I won't."

"Knock yourself out then. But if you got any ideas about stealing yourself a bag full of food before you take off, well... well, I ain't got no way to stop you, but I hope you'll reconsider. Every bit of it's just gonna go to waste *when*...not if... you die out there."

Jason's eye twitched a little; stealing as much food as he could carry before he ran was exactly what he intended to do. "There's a problem with your plan, too, old man."

Benjamin was working on chopping a couple of carrots into the pot of boiling water. "There's a whole lot of problems with it. But go ahead."

"Who's to say you're not gonna turn into one of those monsters before you reach the end of the line? What happens then?"

Benjamin paused, holding his knife still against the end of a carrot just for a tick, but Jason noticed it. "Yeah, suppose I could. Like I told you, it's got a whole lot of problems. Biggest one being it's the only plan I have."

Was there more there? Something he wasn't letting on? Jason wasn't sure, but a faint feeling somewhere deep inside told him there was.

"Tell me what happens when they turn."

"Never actually seen it happen," Benjamin said. "They all just disappeared. Then next time I seen 'em again, they were like they are now."

"And they never did anything to cause it?"

"Not that I know about."

Jason forced himself to think back to his time with The Slaver, despite the way picturing that face made his skin crawl and his balls shrivel at the memory of being lopped off. The Slaver had blamed Jupiter for his situation. What that meant, whether it meant anything at all coming from a brain as scrambled as that one's, Jason had no idea. "So if you turn into one of them things, you're just stuck that way forever then or what?"

Benjamin pulled out a chair on the other end of the table and sat down with a groan and a sigh. "Son, I've told you before I don't have all the answers. I know you may not believe that seeing as I did tell you a little fib that one time...for your own good mind you...but it's the truth. I don't know what happens to 'em. I don't know what's gonna happen to me. But I do know that ain't any of them changed one bit since they turned while I have. Maybe that means something."

"Maybe it doesn't mean shit," Jason said.

"Maybe it don't."

They didn't talk much more for the next hour while the chicken and vegetables boiled. By the time it was ready, the sun had started to set. Another day without a Flip come and gone. Jason shoveled a spoonful of bleach-white chicken into his mouth and barely chewed it before helping it down with a gulp of water. He was famished, and that made it enjoyable, but it was a far cry from tasty. Seasonings, even salt and pepper, weren't anywhere to be found around here. And Jason wasn't sure how good of a cook the old man would have made if he had a whole supermarket at his disposal.

"We should see about making some cheese," Jason said.

"Don't know how."

Instinctively, Jason thought of the internet. But he had left his phone back in Alabama. He wondered if it would even work here if he had it. "Did you know that, where I come from, everyone carries their phone with them in their pocket?"

Jason expected the old man to find this surprising, but he didn't even look up from his bowl.

"Yeah, I know. You ain't the first one from the future to come strolling up here, remember? And why's that what everyone always tries to impress me with, anyway? Eighty years of progress between your time and mine, and the best the world can do is a damn telephone in your pocket? Hell, I never liked calling people anyway. Anything worth saying is worth saying face-to-face. Or writing down in a letter if the person lives a piece away."

Jason sniffed. "They do more than just call people now."

"I figured we'd have put a man on the moon or something by then."

"We did. Long time ago, before I was born."

"Huh," Benjamin said and scratched his broth-stained beard. "Ain't that something. Now see, how come no one ever mentioned that? That's something worth bragging about right there."

"If you say so, old man. Putting those assholes up there never did me any good, that's for sure."

Benjamin slurped loudly at the last few dregs of soup in his bowl, then set it back down on the table. "It any better where you're from?" he asked, wiping his mouth. "Or is everything still just as miserable?"

"It's only gotten worse."

"Yeah," Benjamin said with a sigh. "I figured. Oliver said there was some kind of pandemic going on when he got here. Strolled up with a funny looking mask on his face. I thought he was a doctor or a surgeon at first."

"Who's Oliver?" Jason asked.

"Oliver Lench. He's The Ice Cream Man now. Showed up about nine years ago."

Jason rolled the name over in his mind, trying to figure out why it seemed to mean something to him. Did he know someone by that name? Must have not liked him very much if he did based on the simmer of anger he felt, but that wasn't saying a lot; Jason didn't like anyone.

"What was he like?"

"Sick in the head. Used to diddle kids. Turning into The Ice Cream Man didn't help none neither."

Jason noticed that he'd clenched his fists into balls and wondered why. It wasn't like he cared about the kids. The old man must have noticed, too; Jason saw his eyes narrow a little with misplaced concern.

"I don't know why you're looking at me like that, son. I'm telling you the truth."

Jason shook his head, almost as if to shake the feeling. "It's nothing."

He could feel Benjamin watching him, obviously not very convinced and probably wondering if he was about to snap into a fit of extreme violence. It hadn't happened yet since Jason's return from The Slaver, but he'd made sure that the possibility was never far from the old man's mind.

"Think I'll hit the sack a little early tonight," Benjamin said, standing from the table. "You and I got a lot of work to do tomorrow."

"I've decided I'm taking a rest day tomorrow."

Benjamin didn't turn around, just kept heading for his bedroom. "Oh? That so?" Jason could tell he'd tried to keep the words from sounding like a challenge, but a little of his irritation leaked through anyway.

"We've been going nonstop, old man. Every minute we're not getting tortured to death, anyway. And what for? I've seen the pantry. There's enough food in there to feed us for a year."

Benjamin stopped at the hallway and sighed. "You'll figure out how things work around here eventually, son. But you do whatever you want, I suppose. Just don't blame me when there's nothing to eat. Like I told you the day you got here, starving's a bad way to go."

With that, he ducked into his bedroom and closed and locked the door. For another half hour, Jason stayed at the table, caught up in a vortex of thought that kept pulling him down to the same dark places. The utter silence of the kitchen gave room for voices almost audible to whisper their devilry. Jason closed his eyes against the lantern's flicker and listened. Before long, they lulled him to sleep.

CHAPTER THIRTEEN

Even before his arrival at the farm, Jason's dreams were rarely pleasant. So, when the rays of golden sunshine and cool, soft grass at his feet shimmered into existence, it caught him by surprise. Even more surprising was how vivid this dream became the moment he realized he was dreaming. It came alive in an instant. He could smell the mulch from the flowerbed beside him and felt the sun warming the back of his neck.

The next thing Jason noticed about this dream was that he'd become a kid again. Not just in the sense that he felt like one, with a spirit whose wings the monsters of the world had not yet fully clipped, but in the sense that he had the body of a child, all elbows and knees and not yet half the height he'd reached by nineteen.

He was at his foster parents' home, too, he was pretty sure. One of them anyway. Even if he explored for a while, he probably couldn't have said which one. Between the drugs and the trying to forget (two things that went together nicely), those years were all a blur now. But he still recognized the flamingo lawn ornaments and the screened-in front porch on some deep-buried level.

It was a lot different now, though. All polished up and soaked in sunshine. As Jason noticed the discrepancies, the memories of the true place came back to him one by one. Here, the house was pristine instead of falling apart; the chips and peeled paint on the gnome in the flowerbed were gone; the cracks in the concrete walkway splitting the lawn were all repaired.

He didn't have a lot of time to wonder what it meant before a sound caught his attention. Music—a ways away but getting closer. Jason heard the lyrics to the song in his head even though the music coming from down the street was only a cheerful assortment of instruments. Then, when the sound drew a little closer, he realized it wasn't just in his head. Someone was singing along to the tune.

"Do your ears hang low?
Do they wobble to and fro?
Can you tie 'em in a knot?
Can you tie 'em in a bow?
Can you throw 'em o'er your shoulder
Like a continental soldier?
Do your ears hang low?"

Jason saw a vehicle coming down the street. A white, box-shaped van with a banana split painted on its hood. The driver had his head out the window, belting out the song's second verse for all the neighborhood to hear. Though, looking around, Jason didn't see anyone else out and about.

The ice cream truck drove slowly past each house, nonetheless, giving ample opportunity for the music to lure out anyone who might be inside. Finally, it rolled to a stop in front of the driveway where Jason stood. Still leaning out the window, the driver waved at him while the tune continued to stream from the truck's speakers.

"Howdy there, little buddy! How'd you like something sweet to eat?" He grinned so wide it was comical. His round face beamed like a spotlight was shining on it. Even from across the driveway, Jason could see a literal sparkle in the man's eyes.

He recognized him—both his face and his voice. Or at least he thought he did. But when he tried to search his memory for where he knew this man, his thoughts kept ending up on other things: rainbow sprinkles falling like snow onto vanilla scoops, chocolate syrup dripping down a sugar cone, a maraschino cherry slowly sinking into a spiral of whipped cream.

"Why don't you come see what I've got on the truck today, pal? You can pick out whatever you want. Free of charge!"

Jason stared at him. Alarms rang somewhere in the abyss of his mind, but they were too deep and muffled to heed. For the first time in his entire adult life, true happiness had pierced his soul. The happiness of childhood's earliest days returned, however temporary, in this dream of a sun-soaked suburb where the colors shined like neon and the air smelled like strawberry candy.

With no regard for the feeling that he recognized the plump face still grinning from the open window, he began walking toward the truck.

He'd almost made it to the end of the driveway when his feet flew out from under him. Jason flailed at the empty air, then landed hard on his back. The wind rushed out of his lungs in a sharp huff. Then darkness closed on him.

When Jason opened his eyes (though he didn't remember closing them), he was staring up at wooden rafters. He heard a door slam, then the sound of its bolt turning.

"What the hell are you doing?" Benjamin hissed, whirling on him.

Jason sat up. He started to say something but stopped when a noise outside the house caught his ears. Music. Ice cream truck music. The same tune as in his dream but distorted now and at a lower pitch.

"Just open the goddamn door for him, why don't you?"

"What's happening?" Jason asked, rising to his feet.

"The Flip. Started about five minutes ago. Woke me up when it did, and good thing, too. Now quick, help me barricade the doors."

Still muddled with sleep and confusion, Jason followed the old man to his bedroom and helped him carry out a large wooden chest full of something heavy enough to make lifting it a struggle. They shuffled across the living room with it and dropped it in front of the door.

"Shit!" Benjamin said, sucking at the finger he'd just smashed. He glared at Jason, then put his weight against the chest to press it flush against the door.

"There's a water barrel in the kitchen," he said. "Bring it here."

The music had grown louder by the time Jason returned with the barrel of water in his arms. Through the living room window, the bright yellow beams of headlights cast scattered streams of light across the room. Faintly, he could hear a voice now amidst the music and the engine's rumble. It, too, sounded low and distorted, almost like it had been slowed on a turntable.

"Dooo...yooour...eeeears...haaang...loooooow?

Doo...theeey...wooobble...tooo and froooooo?"

"Hurry up!" Benjamin shouted. Jason broke through his fugue and set the barrel on top of the chest against the door.

Benjamin tested its sturdiness. "That should keep him out. He's not very persistent."

"Who?"

"The Ice Cream Man, damn you. Was the music not enough?"

Jason walked up to the window and peered through. The headlights bounced up and down as the truck rumbled down the bumpy dirt road. In their backsplash, he could just make out the truck's white hood and the banana split painted across it. Except now the paint was peeling, and rings of rust spotted the hood like reddish-brown crop circles.

"I had a dream about him," Jason said.

"Yeah, I know. Had to practically tackle you to wake you up from it. That's how he lures you in."

"I recognized him," Jason whispered. The truck was so close now he could hear the gravel grinding beneath its tires. Its brakes squealed as it pulled to a stop right in front of the house. Its engine sputtered, then died. The headlights faded, and so did the distorted moan of music from its speakers.

"Bullshit," the old man whispered back. "Now keep your head down and stay quiet." Jason moved away from the window.

With the truck's headlights no longer spilling through, it was near total darkness in the house. Jason shuffled over to the old man and stood next to him, facing the dark silhouette of obstacles they'd piled in front of the door.

Rusty hinges screeched outside as the door to the ice cream truck opened. There were pants and groans, then a heavy thud that followed. Jason could hear labored breaths and thundering footfalls approaching.

The doorknob turned, jostling against the lock, and Jason held his breath. When it didn't open, whatever was on the other side began rattling it hard enough to shake the doorframe.

Suddenly, the shaking stopped. Jason heard panting again, even more rapid than before, then the choking sound of swallowed spit that didn't all go down the right pipe followed by smacking lips.

"Ooopppeen up, kiddooos! I got noooo time for gaaaames!"

The voice had the grating quality of silverware in a garbage disposal, with a forced cheerfulness that masked the malice beneath about as well as honey on a shit sandwich. And yet Jason still recognized it from somewhere. Hearing it now without all the sunshine and wistfulness from the dream left him with a cold feeling in his core.

"Just hold what you got, son," Benjamin whispered through the corner of his mouth. "Long as you don't rile him up, he'll leave eventually."

The doorknob turned again, as if the thing on the other side truly believed they might have unlocked it for him. A frustrated moan followed, then the sound of meaty palms slamming against the wood.

"Doooon't make me loooose myyy temper! Papa waaants his snuggles, kiddooooos!"

There was a pause, followed by the sound of receding footsteps. For just an instant, Jason thought he was leaving. Then he heard a grunt and two rapid, heavy steps followed by the crash of a massive body against the door.

A cry of pain and frustration came after the thundering boom failed to breach the door. Then heavy panting again and a few snotty sniffles.

"Come on nooow, Ezekiel. Let your papa innnn."

Jason felt the fear rising in his stomach freeze into solid ice, and every hair on his body went rigid. He wanted to run, but there was nowhere to go, and he'd hunted enough rabbits to know that the ones who lost their nerve and broke cover were always more likely to get cut down.

Another jiggle of the doorknob. Another groaning whimper and more heavy hands slapping the door hard enough to shake it. Then Jason heard a roar that rose in volume like a sawblade winding up and the sound of footsteps crashing away.

"He's leaving," Benjamin whispered.

The ice cream truck door opened and slammed closed. Its engine turned and sputtered. Its tires peeled away in a pattering spray of gravel. Jason hurried to the living room window, hugging the wall and peering around the edge of the pane.

"Get away from there!" the old man hissed, but Jason didn't listen.

He saw taillights growing steadily more distant down the road. Just as he started to breathe again, he saw a second set of lights cast bright red rays into the dark stalks of corn on either side of the road.

Brake lights.

He heard the grind of gears and watched the truck swerve in reverse off the road and into the cornfield. The gears ground again, and its tires spun in the mud before the truck lurched forward. It fishtailed a little, then its engine snarled as soon as the wheels straightened. Jason squinted against the headlights that were bouncing erratically as the truck barreled down the road.

"Get back!" Benjamin yelled.

Jason took a few steps back. Slower than he should have, maybe, had his muscles not been so gummed up by bewilderment. The engine's howl reached a piercing volume just before the wall in front of him seemed to detonate in a shower of splinters and plaster.

The impact shook the living room floor hard enough to make Jason lose his balance. He fell and scooted away from the front tire of the truck that was now spinning against the hardwood with a rubbery whine.

Dislodged components in the engine knocked and clanged. The smell of gasoline and motor oil filled the room. His back against the far wall, Jason watched through the clouds of smoke spilling from its hood as the truck's crumpled door shuddered open.

A pair of tree-trunk legs swung out, sending a shower of safety glass cubes onto the living room floor. Jason saw tattered, white cargo pants stretched so tight around engorged calves they were ripping at the seams. The obese man grunted as he squeezed himself out the door. A mess of curly, ginger hair poked out, framing a doughy face split in half by a stream of blood. He turned his crazed, green eyes to where Jason sat and ran a swollen tongue across his busted bottom lip.

"Run, you idiot!" Benjamin screamed without turning around as he beat feet out of the living room. Jason scrambled up and followed him, passing the old man by the time they reached the kitchen table. The back door in the kitchen was bolted and locked, and Jason hurried to get them both unlatched. He could hear footsteps from the living room, thudding and unsteady and getting closer.

"Hurry up!"

Jason flung open the door and took a step outside.

Only one step, though. When he saw a burlap face bristling with straw and the smell of smoke pricked his nostrils, Jason threw himself back inside and slammed the door closed.

The Scarecrow's pitchfork hit the door the same instant it shut. All three spikes pierced the wood. Jason stared up at their rusted tips for a heartbeat before turning back to the old man.

"Now what do we..."

The question died on his lips when he saw a lumbering figure enter the kitchen. In the mixing glow of moonlight from the kitchen window and headlights from the living room, The Ice Cream Man's pallid face beamed. His left arm, which looked more like a flipper with all the man's flab, was clearly dislocated at the elbow based on the way it hung. But a toothy grin still stretched his face, and his other arm worked at the bulge in his pants, teasing it through the fabric with sausage-like fingers.

"Nooow looook whaaat you kiddoooos made me doooo…"

Jason's eyes darted to the block of knives on the kitchen counter. Much swifter than the monster could move to stop him, he dove for them. He yanked the first one his fingers found from the block—a carving knife almost as long as his forearm—while The Ice Cream Man broke out into a cackling laugh.

"No!" Benjamin screamed, recognizing what Jason meant to do. But Jason barely heard him. All he could think about was the thing that looked like a walrus standing on its hind flippers and the psychotic lust in his eyes; the rotten milk smell of his breath as he leered closer and the maddening way everything about this moment smothered Jason with déjà vu.

Not willing to live this experience another heartbeat longer, Jason drove the knife into his own ribcage and let the sharpened steel make sure that beat didn't happen.

Oliver's Transgression

Squealing Jimmy's BBQ was the most popular restaurant in Highwater. The kind of place you'd never find empty on a Friday afternoon even with the virus still going around and all the mandates in effect. Not a dog's chance.

But it was empty now.

This wasn't something that would've normally bothered Oliver Lench; he wasn't there to socialize. But the trouble of it—the reason his gaping mouth hung open while BBQ beans dripped from his fork—was that the restaurant had been bustling with people just a second ago.

Now, not even the talking heads on the TVs were left, the screens going silent and lifeless the same time as the rest of the place. The only person still there besides Oliver was a redheaded woman sitting across from him. And she had not been there before.

She looked mesmerizing in a way that made her appearing there on the other side of the booth all the more baffling.

She wasn't nearly young enough to stir Oliver's attractions, but most men would have found her stunning: a fantasy of feminine perfection brought to life. Sunset-colored waves of hair spilled across her elegant shoulders. Eyes as green as Heaven's meadows transfixed him with their unblinking stare.

"Hello, Oliver."

"What...where did you come from?" he blubbered.

"That doesn't matter. What matters is why I'm here."

"Oh yeah?" With some effort, Oliver broke from her gaze and darted his eyes around the restaurant one more time. Where the hell had everyone gone? There was no way they could have all left so suddenly without him noticing. He glanced at the glass of beer next to his plate, but it was only half empty. Oliver rarely drank to the point of blacking out anymore, and, when he did, it took a whole lot more than that.

"I have a question for you," the woman said.

"Huh?"

"How many people do you think you've killed in your lifetime, Oliver?"

"*Huh?*" Oliver blinked at her. Surely he'd misheard her. Hell, *surely she wasn't real.*

"I asked how many people you think you've killed. It's not a rhetorical question. I'm genuinely curious if you know what the number is."

Oliver huffed. "I don't know what you're talking about. Zero. That's the number."

"Hmm," the woman said and shook her head. "That's not true."

Oliver set his hands against the table and began the slow process of sliding his bulky body out of the booth. "I don't know what's going on here, but I'm leaving."

"No. You're going to stay."

Oliver laughed nervously. "You're a crazy bitch, aren't you? Well...have a nice life, crazy bitch." He leaned and swung his right leg out of the booth...

...then recoiled when he looked down and saw it dangling over empty air. The table and the benches bolted to it hung suspended in the sky, so high above whatever lay below that all Oliver could see beneath him was a fog of clouds.

Still sitting across the now levitating booth, the woman closed her eyes and took a deep breath. "Don't you love how clear the air is up here?"

"This isn't real," Oliver said. With a trembling hand, he picked up his fork. It slipped from his fingers as soon as it was past the edge of the table even before he'd meant to drop it. He watched it plummet out of sight into the clouds below.

"It's quite real, Oliver. Feel free to test it yourself if you're still not convinced. I don't mind."

"You want me to die?"

The woman shrugged. "Death isn't going to have the same permanence for you anymore."

"What is this?" Oliver was growing more flustered by the second. "Who are you?"

"My name is Eden. And this is the consequence of your actions."

"I...What are you talking about?" She fixed him in a gaze that made it impossible to look away. Oliver felt like a suspect on trial. Like he was facing his judge.

"I want to go back to my previous question, Oliver. Except this time, I want you to think about it a little harder. How many people do you think you've killed?"

At this point, if there'd been a dozen bodies buried in his backyard, he probably would've come clean. But Oliver truly did not know what she expected from him. He had committed a lot of wrongs in his life, but murder wasn't one of them.

"There's more than one way to kill a person, you know?" Eden said, as though she could read his thoughts. "Killing their soul is the same as killing their body. In ways, it's even worse."

Oliver blinked and swallowed. He felt the blood rush to his ears as they started to ring. "I didn't..."

"There's no use denying it. I know everything you've ever done, Oliver. All your secret sins. So, I'm going to ask you one last time. How many children did you *murder?*"

This time, Oliver couldn't help but picture their faces. Little boys and girls whose names, for the most part, he'd forgotten. He saw their snaggle-toothed smiles and eyes gleaming with innocent wonder. They were more beautiful to him than the woman in front of him—than any man or woman—could ever be. Yet as he watched those smiles fade one by one and those sparkling eyes go dim, icy fingers wrapped around his heart. It felt like something he understood but had never really experienced before. Like shame.

"You sentenced every one of them to the slowest death imaginable," Eden said. "So far, only one has succumbed. Charles Hopper. He committed suicide nine years ago at age seventeen. But you'll be to blame when the rest pass, too. Because even if they die a natural death, their lives all ended the moment they met you."

Oliver gawked at her. His thoughts kept skipping from one question to another. "What is going on?" he asked, at last settling on one.

But Eden didn't answer him. "And the fourteen children—that's how many there were, in case you didn't keep count—they are only the beginning. There isn't time or words to explain all the ripples of destruction your evil has caused."

Oliver took another stomach-turning glance at the seemingly bottomless drop just a slip away. He'd always been scared of heights. He wondered if she'd known this, like she somehow knew the rest. "How are you doing this? It's not possible."

Eden glared at him. A gust of cold wind lifted her hair and cut straight through clothing Oliver had never intended to wear at such an altitude. Viridescent flames seemed to leap within her eyes. "You're focusing on the wrong things, Oliver. Years from now, centuries maybe, when you're thinking back on this conversation for the ten thousandth time, you're going to wish you'd focused on what mattered. Honestly, you should think of being here right now as an act of mercy. One you don't deserve."

"I don't know what you want from me," Oliver said.

"Repentance."

"I'm sorry!" he shouted with no hesitation. "Is that what you want? I'm sorry, and I'll never do it again!"

Eden shook her head while she watched him blubber. "You're not being genuine, Oliver."

Tears stung Oliver's eyes. A surge of the rage he'd always been so prone to shot through him. "How the hell am I supposed to be genuine when you're doing all this?"

"Because if your repentance was real, you'd beg me to kill you for what you've done."

As he sat there trying to make sense of what she'd said, of what was happening, a thought struck Oliver. A theory that might explain at least a little of this madness. "You were one of them, weren't you?"

The woman's frown shot this down right away. "It's disappointing you don't even remember their faces. No. I'm not one of your victims. But you did destroy the life of one like me. I'm willing to bet you remember him."

Oliver wasn't sure what she meant, but a memory did surface. The image of a boy with pale skin and dark brown eyes. Ezekiel. That's what his name had been. Oliver remembered how it felt when the boy first arrived at the orphanage where he'd worked as a counselor. The mixing fumes of wonder and lust that would envelop him every time he was near the child.

"That boy had a purpose on this earth," Eden said. "When you killed his soul, you destroyed that purpose, too. You didn't just murder an angel, Oliver. You turned one into a demon."

"So what?" Oliver said. Terrified or not, he was running out of patience. And faking remorse had clearly got him nowhere. "What are you going to do about it? Kill me?"

The way she looked at him then almost made Oliver wish she would. "There is a place that shouldn't exist but does," Eden said. "Created by the sins of someone a lot like you. Someone who also saw Heaven in human form and defiled it to feed his own lust. Because of what you've done, this place is going to claim you, Oliver. What happens then is up to you."

"Yeah? And what if I don't want to go? Is that part up to me, too?"

But by the time Oliver got the words out, the woman was no longer there. The din of conversation and clinking silverware that had gone suddenly silent earlier returned with no warning. The clouds beneath his dangling feet turned back to a solid floor.

Oliver was dumbstruck, but only for an instant. From the corner of his eye, he spotted something strange out the window next to his booth. Right there at the end of the parking lot, where Gibson Street should have been, was instead an old dirt road cutting through a cornfield.

Oliver rubbed his eyes. Not only was the road still there when he opened them again, it had taken on a different appearance entirely. Except *appearance* wasn't quite the right word, Oliver decided; the road and the corn still looked just the same as before. What had changed was how they both spoke to him now.

With his head craned so that his eyes never had to leave the window, Oliver slid out of the booth. He stumbled across the restaurant toward the exit, bumping into tables along the way and drawing glares from the other patrons.

Oliver couldn't have cared less. The fact that he wouldn't be able to see the road again until he was out the door bothered him much more than any stranger's judgment. Infinitely more. He hurried as fast as his bulk would allow, whimpering with anticipation.

When he made it out the restaurant's swing doors and the road came back into view, Oliver began to cry and laugh at the same time. The beauty he somehow found in its mundane appearance—ordinary in every way except for its location and the fact that it hadn't been there before—defied all reason. It lit up his eyes and washed him in ecstasy. Paradise was where that road led. There was not a doubt in his mind.

Two minutes later, a young waitress wearing a maroon apron burst out the doors of Squealing Jimmy's BBQ, an unpaid bill with nearly half the menu on it crumpled in her fist.

She scanned the parking lot for the large man who'd just skipped his tab, planning to run him down and, at the very least, embarrass the hell out of him. But he was nowhere to be seen.

"Asshole," the waitress muttered. Then, when a strange feeling like static in the air sent a shiver through her, she hurried back inside.

Ezekiel's Mission

Ezekiel Hartman wrapped his wool blanket around his body and did his best to get comfortable on the metal park bench. He'd been sleeping on an old mattress behind the dumpsters of Brookstone Apartments until the property manager called the cops and had him trespassed. Sleeping on the bench had taken some getting used to, but at least the drugs helped.

He could feel them swimming through his blood and into his brain already. A warm, welcome embrace. The Puerto Rican gangbanger he'd bought the dope from had sold it to him as heroin, but Ezekiel knew that was bullshit. There might have been a little H in there, but fentanyl is what it was. Far from feeling cheated, that suited Ezekiel just fine.

He closed his eyes against the yellow-orange beams of a streetlight that was closer than he wished it was and let the night breeze flow over his sweaty skin. For a moment sure to be too brief, he found peace.

Sleep would bring its own kind of peace, too, so long as it didn't bring dreams. There were a variety of dreams that came to him, but they always repeated. Awake to remember them, he knew each one by heart. Yet asleep and dreaming, it always felt like the first time.

He dreamed of Oliver Lench. That was the worst one. So much fear and shame came with it and never dissipated quickly when he woke.

He dreamed of the life he should have had. One where his parents didn't both die of cancer before he was old enough to walk in the cruelest twist of "what are the odds?" one could imagine.

And he dreamed of the school bus. He dreamed of it careening off the highway. Tumbling down the mountain. Bodies flying through the glass. That dream always brought its own flavor of shame. Shame for the mission he felt doomed to fail.

"They'll send another," he muttered half-asleep. The words came out whispered and slurred. Like a drunkard's midnight prayer.

It was wrong, what he was doing. Much worse, it was *dangerous*. Those sent to earth—sent straight into the teeth of trials and temptations the likes of which they've never known—had only their mission to guide them. Abandon that mission, and there was no limit to how far an angel could fall. Already, Ezekiel could feel himself beginning to not care about them. Each time he thought of that bus and all the lives that would be lost, it hurt a little less. The whole of humanity seemed less and less important to him with every day that passed. All they'd ever done was hurt him anyway.

Though even with his moral compass shifting the further from his mission he strayed, Ezekiel knew that last part wasn't entirely true. There'd been a few good people in his life. The foster parents he lived with for six months when he was eight, Alice and Hank Chesterfield, had been kind. Ezekiel used to pray that they would adopt him, but then Hank got into a car accident that put him in the hospital for a while, and the bills sank their ability to provide for another hungry mouth.

Kim Smith, one of the volunteers at Roosevelt Boys' Home, had always been kind, too. She used to play board games with him for hours on end. At the time, he wished that she would adopt him. But, looking back, he realized the girl—who still had a year of study left before she graduated college—hadn't quite been the adult she'd seemed like to him.

Then there was Jason Baker. Jason was the only boy at the orphanage who had ever been Ezekiel's long-term friend. A forever kid, just like him, growing less and less likely to ever find a home the older and less adoptable they both got until the notion eventually became a regretful dream. Ezekiel had always admired Jason's strength. Even when Oliver Lench came into their lives, he never saw the kid crack.

There'd been a time when Ezekiel thought Oliver was one of the good ones, too. He had such a booming laugh and goofy smile—both so infectious there at first. And he would often bring ice cream back after his lunch break from the Baskin-Robins down the road. Enough for every boy at the orphanage.

God, he just wanted to stop thinking about it all. To stop thinking entirely. He should have been barely conscious by now, floating on a sea of chemical bliss. He wished he could have blamed the dealer for selling him shitty dope, but Ezekiel knew the truth; the drugs just weren't working like they used to. Where before they doused it like a bucket of water, now they only dulled the pain.

He focused on the sounds of the city as if the erratic melody could soothe him. It was better than silence at least. Lately, strange things had been coming to fill the silence.

He could faintly hear their voices now despite the hum of distant traffic and barking dogs. Little whispers in his head. Some proposed he end his life; there was more than enough fentanyl left to do it, they encouraged. If Ezekiel was going to listen to any of the demons that circled him like vultures, he knew he should listen to these.

The things the rest proposed were much more terrible.

CHAPTER FOURTEEN

The dead don't have nightmares. Not even those destined for resurrection. So, when Benjamin opened his eyes and saw a ruinous hellscape all around him, it confused him at first more than anything.

He had most certainly died. The Ice Cream Man had smashed his head like an egg as soon as he was done getting his rocks off. Which meant that The Flip should have ended, and he should have been waking up on the kitchen floor where it happened, not in a pile of soot and charred wood.

Then he noticed the cast iron stove, sitting there in a heap of ash with the full length of its chimney exposed, and it hit him. This *was* his kitchen.

Benjamin's stomach roiled. He staggered to his feet and scanned the smoldering wreckage for the son of a bitch who'd caused this. It didn't take long to spot him. He was practically right at Benjamin's feet, sleeping off the cardiac surgery he'd given himself with the knife still clutched in his hands like a teddy bear. Benjamin stormed over to him and kicked him in the leg.

"Wake up, asshole!"

Jason startled awake and squirmed onto his back, holding the knife out in a defensive posture. He lowered it only a little when he realized it was Benjamin standing over him.

"Look what you did!" Benjamin seethed.

Jason sat up and looked around, his eyebrows scrunching as he did. "Did they fucking burn the place down?"

"Wow. You should have been a detective, son."

Jason glared at him. "How's that my fault, old man? You said if we just kept quiet, he'd leave."

"Because you killed yourself!" Benjamin felt like throttling his neck, but he kept his hands clenched at his side. "Don't you get it yet? You don't get to cheat this place. There ain't no easy way out. Hell, if that's all it took to keep 'em from dragging you away somewhere and carving pieces off you for a week, don't you think that's what I would have told you to do from the start?"

"You could have told me not to, you know."

Benjamin snorted and spat a wad of phlegm into the ash. "Yeah, as if that would have done any good. I was better off just not putting the idea in your head."

"I thought I made it clear what would happen if you didn't stop hiding things from me, old man," Jason said.

Benjamin could tell he was in no mood for this lecture to go on any longer; Jason's grip on the knife had tightened, and his jaw was clenched. Benjamin didn't care, was about to keep ripping into him anyway, when he noticed something behind the man's stupid head.

He almost couldn't believe his eyes. It looked like some kind of giant totem pole or ungodly sculpture. The pink carcasses of every pig on the farm formed its roughly dome-shaped base. The goats came next, bound with barbed wire around a charred beam from the house that was buried in the center of the pig pile to form a pillar of bloody fur, hooves, and horns. Dangling from every limb that jutted from this pillar were his chickens, all plucked naked and strung up by different lengths of twine nooses. Their feathers lay scattered across the ground like leaves that had fallen from this grotesque tree.

With sickening certainty of what he'd see, Benjamin turned his attention to the garden and the fields. It was just as he'd feared. They'd all been scorched to the roots. For as far into the distance as his old eyes could make out, there was only cinders and smoldering earth.

"You ruined us," he said, his voice a feeble croak.

Except Benjamin didn't know how true that really was. The big idiot wasn't the first one on the farm to off himself. And while trying to cheat the Avengers out of their fun never went unpunished, it had also never provoked a reaction anywhere near this extreme.

Slowly, Jason seemed to realize the extent of the crisis. He kept staring and blinking at the tower of carcasses like he expected it to have disappeared each time he opened his eyes.

And maybe it would, Benjamin thought, with a tiny flare of hope. Maybe The Flip hadn't actually ended yet, and this was still some upside-down, ruinous version of the farm that would revert back to normal soon enough. But that was an empty hope. He had been here long enough to know the difference just from the charge in the air.

"I recognized him," Jason said, still staring at the tower.

"The hell are you talking about?"

"The Ice Cream Man. I know him from somewhere."

"Bullshit," Benjamin said. But the ball of dread in his stomach started to grow. This wasn't normal. Not even by this farm's deranged standards. They had killed livestock before. They'd ransacked the house before, too. It's why he was always so careful about rationing the food and keeping inventory high. But nothing like this had ever happened. Nothing even close to the literal scorched earth they'd left behind this time.

"What do you mean you know him from somewhere?"

Jason shook his head. "I don't know. Something about his voice. His face, too. I've seen him before."

It was probably just another one of Oliver's tricks. He had all kinds of clever ways of luring you into his arms. Ways of messing with your head. But the buzzing in Benjamin's nerves just kept intensifying. With the smoking ruins of every comfort he'd managed to claw from this cursed ground stinging his eyes, it felt as though the man in front of him was just as cursed.

"He raped you anyway, you know." Benjamin spat. "If that's what you were trying to avoid with that stunt you pulled, it didn't work."

It was a lie; ironically, The Ice Cream Man didn't like it cold. But Benjamin enjoyed the sickly look that passed over Jason's face when he said it. He deserved that. Not only for what he'd caused, but for all the threats he'd been making lately, too.

"There's something going on here," Jason said. Benjamin barely heard him, wasn't sure if it was even meant for him to hear. Jason's eyes were still fixed on the statue of livestock, but it didn't look like they were actually seeing it anymore.

"You're shell-shocked, son," Benjamin said. Yet somewhere deep in his bones, he felt it too. Something wasn't right. They'd pissed this place off somehow, and it wasn't just a knife to the ribcage that'd done it. "Help me. We need to salvage as much of this meat as we can."

Benjamin started walking through the ash toward the carcasses. Jason shook his trance and followed him.

If they worked fast, maybe they could get a good bit of the animals butchered before dark. As for how they'd preserve the meat with the curing house and all his supplies now a heap of rubble, Benjamin didn't have any idea. At least it would keep their bellies full until it turned. That would have to do for now.

But when a breeze carried the tower's putrid scent to his nostrils, Benjamin realized that even this wasn't going to be an option. A few more steps and the details he'd been unable to see at first came into focus. The entire tower was crawling with maggots. The carcasses were already mottled with shades of green and brown, and the stomachs of the pigs and goats were all bloated to the point of bursting.

"What happened?" Jason asked, walking up beside him. He took a deep sniff of the foul air around the tower and crinkled his nose.

Benjamin shook his head. *He* felt like the one who was shell-shocked now. "Either we were asleep for weeks or..." He wasn't sure how to finish the thought. The ringing in his ears and the ball in his throat made it hard to think clearly. "Or they spoiled them somehow."

"Now what?"

Benjamin didn't have an answer. With every morsel of meat rotten and larva-ridden, the tower of carcasses seemed even more mocking than before.

As if on cue (and, knowing this farm, it probably was), the first twinge of morning hunger cramped his stomach.

There's a lot of bad ways to go on this farm, he remembered telling Jason the day he arrived. *But not many are worse than starving.*

CHAPTER FIFTEEN

Jason tossed and turned on the hard ground, attempting to find some position that was bearable. He and the old man had tried to clear the area of rocks before laying down a bed of foliage, but there were still pebbles that they'd missed, and the leaves and the grass stalks he lay on pricked his skin.

They'd fastened some of the bigger branches together to form a lean-to, but the wind cut straight through it. Jason could only imagine how little it would do to stop a driving rain, and the distant flash of lightning told him he might find out soon.

"We'll rebuild," the old man had said. "We've got timber all around us and every tool we need." Jason didn't try very hard to hide the fact he had different plans.

Why he hadn't left already, he wasn't quite sure. Lying on the bare ground listening to the old man snore sure wasn't doing anything for him. Not like a deep-dish pizza was going to sprout up from the ashes any moment either. Jason's stomach protested being teased with such a thought, and he rolled over yet again, as if all the little rocks would feel better poking against his left side this time.

If he was going to run—and he definitely was—there was no better time than now, while he still had some fumes left in the tank. Yet the dark wall of trees to the west, scantly illuminated by the waning moon, seemed menacing. He should have left while there was still daylight. Now, waiting until morning looked like his best bet.

Not a very good bet, but the best one he could find. The old man swore up and down that there was nothing out there. Nothing but an endless forest. And Jason didn't like his prospects of finding something to eat out there very much either; it was just as likely he'd end up poisoning himself as it was he'd find something edible.

What drove him more than the hunger in his belly was the certainty that Benjamin was lying about...*something*. Jason couldn't say what, but whatever it was, he was going to go find it.

"Why do you care if I leave?" Jason had asked just as the sun was setting. The old man had been beating around the bush all day, dropping remarks here and there that were anything but subtle.

"I need your help, son," he'd said. "We can rebuild this place, I'm telling you. We can get a garden going again. I'm sure there's seeds and roots the fire didn't destroy. But if you go running off into the woods like a spooked horse, then I'm gonna be left to do it all by myself."

Maybe it'd been true. Or maybe there was some other reason the old man didn't want him venturing too far. Maybe there was something out there he didn't want him to find.

Daylight seemed so far away with all the stars smattered across a coal-black sky. Gazing up at them, he wondered if they were watching him, too. A stupid thought—he'd never paid much attention in school, but he knew what stars were. Yet tonight, it did feel like they were staring back. It made him want to cover his face in shame.

You deserve this, he could almost hear them whisper. In the utter silence where not even a breeze stirred and no living creature chirped, he was sure he'd heard it. They were billions (trillions? Hell if he knew) of miles away, yet he swore he could hear the hum of them blazing. And voices within the hum, too, most just shy of discernible.

It was maddening. The rocks and pine needles jabbing into his back were maddening. The hunger, and the smell of rot from that grotesque art exhibit just outside their shelter, and the way the old man snored like a chainsaw were all maddening. And, little by little, the dark unknown started to look less frightening.

CHAPTER SIXTEEN

Benjamin woke at dawn's first light to find exactly what he'd expected to. The bed of foliage next to his—well-flattened by all the tossing and turning Jason had done all night—was empty. He hobbled out from underneath the lean-to and took an obligatory look around, already knowing he wouldn't see anything. Maybe a trail of boot prints beating feet for the forest, but that was about the best he could hope for.

"Stupid bastard," he said, shaking his head. Lord knows how long it would take him to finally come wandering back with his tail between his legs. Benjamin himself had spent months out there in the early days. As useless as the man seemed to be, it wasn't hard to imagine him getting himself lost and staying gone a lot longer than that. Starving to death, thirsting, freezing, and dying in The Flip over and over again in search of something that Benjamin had told him a thousand times didn't exist.

To be fair, he couldn't blame Jason for not trusting him. There *were* secrets that he'd hidden. But the woods weren't one of them, and the idea of having to tackle the mountain of work before him all by himself made Benjamin blame him anyway.

Food was the first order of business. Any plans for rebuilding the house would have to be put on hold until he had a sustainable way to keep from starving. For now, he needed an immediate solution, sustainable or not; the hunger gnawing at his stomach had grown longer teeth overnight, and he was starting to feel faint.

Fortunately, Benjamin had prepared for a situation like this. All over the farm, there were caches of supplies he had buried in the ground. Canned goods, which would be the first thing he went for, but also seeds and tools. If there was one good thing about Jason bolting, it was that Benjamin wouldn't have to give up the location of these caches.

There was one buried near the house...well, where the house *used* to be. A food cache that Benjamin replenished every few years to make sure the contents wouldn't be spoiled if he ever needed them. Last time he'd filled and reburied the crate, he remembered putting in canned corn, carrots, potatoes, and lima beans as well as four cans of jerky. The jerky, in particular, was something he'd have to make last. With no prospects for starting his herds over again, it might be the last meat he'd ever eat.

Getting it out of the ground was the next problem. Benjamin spent a few minutes rummaging through the ashes of his barn, kicking over the charred piles with his boots to see if anything could be salvaged, but the fire had burned the handles off all his shovels and hoes. There were emergency tools buried in a cache four hundred steps east of the well, but that was a catch-22 situation, wasn't it? He realized that maybe he hadn't thought that one through all the way. Then again, he hadn't counted on those monsters burning the entire farm to the ground either. Every time he thought about this severe escalation, what it might mean, a swell of dread tightened his throat.

He'd have to manage without a shovel, Benjamin decided. The crate was only buried three or four feet deep. He'd probably bust his fingers up a bit, but he'd get down to it eventually. Though it did leave no room for mistakes when it came to getting the cache's location right; the last thing Benjamin wanted to do was spend the next hour digging in the wrong spot. He wandered around the charred skeleton of the house until he was sure he'd found the northeast corner, then he took fifteen measured paces straight east. The horn of a rock stuck up from the ground where his last footfall landed. Six paces in the direction it pointed was where he needed to dig.

Benjamin double-checked his steps before dropping to his knees. At least the ground was soft. And a long, pointy rock he spotted nearby made the work even easier. Still, it took him a while before he thumped against the top of the crate. His arms were cramping by then, and he was running on fumes of energy.

He dug out the edges of the crate a little more until he could get his hands around it, then strained and lifted with his legs. Slowly, it slid out of the ground amidst a shower of dirt clumps. Benjamin set it down by the edge of the hole and collapsed beside it. He laid there in the grass for a minute—just long enough to catch his breath—before hunger overruled exhaustion.

Using the same rock that'd been his shovel as a crowbar, he set about prying open the crate. It took a little doing, but the nails finally gave. Benjamin peeled open the lid the rest of the way and tossed it aside. Four rows of mason jars lined its bottom, their brass lids catching the sunlight like gold in a treasure chest. Benjamin smiled as his mouth began to water.

But his smile quickly faded. He spotted the mold in the cans of corn first. Its gray-green color stuck out against the yellow kernels. The jar was swimming with it. All of them were, he realized. Even the strips of jerky were coated in a motley fuzz.

For a while, Benjamin just stared blankly at the jars. Then finally he screamed and heaved the entire crate into the air. Glass shattered when it landed. The jars' rotten contents leaked out onto the ground.

They couldn't have all gone bad so quickly. It'd barely been a year and a half since he buried those jars, and he'd double-checked the seals on all of them. He thought of the livestock—how quickly they had rotted, too—and felt his head start to swim. Benjamin lifted his eyes to the cloudless sky still hazed with smoke from yesterday's fire. Was this *her* doing? Was she up there, watching him unravel, wondering if this would be the time he broke?

"I won't do it!" Benjamin shouted. "You hear me? I won't do it!"

When the heavens offered no reply, Benjamin began to weep. He shrank to the ground and curled up in a ball, rocking and crying and clutching himself. It took a while, but eventually, he cried himself to sleep. Or passed out from fatigue and hunger. Either way, darkness descended, and he slipped into a familiar dream. A dream of her and the paradise she'd offered.

A dream of Eden.

CHAPTER SEVENTEEN

Jason tilted his canteen and downed a swallow of water. It wasn't enough to fully quench his thirst, but he had to make what was left last. He'd counted on being able to refill it by now. He thought streams were supposed to be everywhere in the forest. So far, he hadn't seen a single one.

It would be dark soon. The light that dappled the forest floor was starting to grow dimmer, and the air had already cooled. Jason debated whether he should stop for the night or keep going. Crashing around in the dark seemed like a good way to break an ankle. He imagined it'd be a good way to get lost, too, then figured you couldn't really get lost when you don't know where you're going to begin with.

When he happened upon a large, hollowed-out log big enough for him to squeeze inside, Jason made his decision. What settled it was that stopping now meant he'd have a little daylight left to forage the area for food. He'd choked down a few horribly bitter acorns earlier, but they had irritated his stomach more than they satisfied it.

At the last flicker of daylight, just as the forest began to fade to tones of black and gray, Jason stumbled into a small clearing with patches of wild onions growing near its edges. He groaned; he'd always hated onions. But still he tore them from the earth and shoveled them into his mouth greens and all as fast as he could manage. His stomach roiled by the time darkness fell, and he had a bad feeling that the onions would end up upsetting it just as much as the acorns. At least it wasn't empty anymore.

It took him a while to find his way back to the fallen log in the dark. At one point, he almost gave up and resigned himself to sleeping at the base of a tree. But the wind was picking up, and it felt like there might be rain in the air. At last, he practically tripped over it. Jason had planned on lining the bottom of the log with some moss, but his odds of finding any in the dark weren't worth the risk of getting turned around again. So he grabbed his pack to use as a pillow and pushed himself feet-first into the log's pitch-black opening, hoping there weren't any snakes or spiders who'd claimed it first.

As soon as Jason had wriggled the full length of his body into the hollow space, the entire day's buildup of exhaustion hit him all at once. The wood inside the log had grown soft from decay, and it made for a suitable mattress. Even its wet, earthy smell soothed him. In a matter of minutes, Jason was fast asleep.

A boom of thunder was what woke him, though the first thing Jason noticed was the pool of water he was laying in. It came down in torrents outside the log and flowed in through the opening.

Jason felt a sudden wave of panic as the claustrophobia of the confined space seized him, and he clawed his way out of the log. The downpour outside was both deafening and blinding when combined with the darkness. It overwhelmed his senses and left him feeling disoriented. For a long time, he just stood there, unsure what to do. Going back to sleep wasn't an option. Traveling in these conditions wasn't either. He was still weighing his choices when a flash of nearby lightning brought the forest into momentary illumination.

As a crack of thunder followed it, Jason nearly jumped out of his skin. Someone had been standing in front of him. No more than three or four feet away. He froze and wondered if they'd seen him, too. He listened but heard no sound aside from the cascade of rain.

They *must* have seen him. In fact, that had to be why they were here in the first place. Jason decided to run.

"Hello?" a voice in the darkness said, freezing him again. "Whoever's there, I don't mean you any harm."

Jason didn't move. It was going to take a whole lot more than that to convince him. He knew he should run, should have already been doing it. But intrigue kept him rooted for a moment longer.

The voice sounded nothing like any of the monsters he'd encountered so far. And while the elements made it difficult to say for certain, Jason didn't think The Flip had happened either. There was always a distinct feeling in the air when it did, and he didn't feel it now.

"I'm going to turn my light on," the voice in the darkness said. "That way I can see you, and you can see me. Is that alright?"

It was a man's voice, but a timid one. Jason could hear the waver in it; unless this was another trick, the guy sounded just as scared as he was. A few more moments of standing there in the dark downpour, and he decided to take the chance. "Go on."

Jason heard the jingle of what sounded like keys, then a clicking noise. A halo of white light cut through the wall of rain.

Jason shielded his eyes with his forearm. Behind the beam of light, he could just make out the dark shape of a man, but that was all. "Your turn, asshole!" he yelled.

The man tilted the light up so that it shined on his face. The haze of rain still blurred Jason's view, but he could see more details now. The man was short, or shorter than him at least, with a thin build and a face so small his glasses took up the bulk of it. He wore what looked like some kind of gray jumpsuit.

"Who the fuck are you?" Jason yelled over the wind.

"Dr. Damien Winters."

Jason recognized that name. Benjamin had told it to him. It was the name of the man who became The Scientist.

"I'm not what you think I am," the man said, as if he had seen the change in Jason's expression.

"No? What are you then?"

Jason caught a glimpse of a smile through the rain. "Still figuring that one out myself, I'm afraid. But if you'll follow me, I'll tell you more. I've got shelter. And food."

The thought of running crossed Jason's mind again. So did the thought of the knife in his pack. What did he have to lose, though? His life was a boomerang now. If he did something dumb and threw it away, it would come right back to him.

"Lead the way," Jason finally said. "Just know that if you try anything, I'm going to stick a knife in your back. Is that clear?"

"Clear as rain," Damien said. Jason couldn't tell if he was joking or not; at the moment, the sheets of rain still obscured almost everything from sight. But if it was a joke, Damien didn't wait for a laugh. He turned and took off walking. For a few seconds, Jason watched his light begin to disappear into the deluge. Then he swiped his pack off the ground and started jogging to catch up.

Jason didn't know what to expect at the end of the trek through the woods that the man in the gray jumpsuit led him on, but a bunker in the ground had been nowhere on his radar. A cylinder with a lid on top of it like a manhole cover jutted up a few inches from the forest floor. Had Damien—if that was even his real name—not stopped in front of it, prompting Jason to stop, too, he would've tripped over it.

He watched as Damien knelt and twisted open the lid, holding his flashlight between his teeth while he worked. He struggled to lift it out of place; even through the jumpsuit, Jason could tell that the man was skin and bones. He reminded himself not to underestimate him but couldn't help thinking how easy it would be to snap him in half like a No. 2 pencil.

"Would you like to go first, or shall I?" Damien asked, gesturing his light toward the circular hole leading straight down into the ground. Jason could see a ladder made of welded metal that disappeared into the darkness.

"You first," Jason said. In fact, he hadn't decided yet if he was even going to follow. He could wait until the man was a few rungs down, then trap him inside. He didn't know exactly what that would accomplish, but it seemed like it might be a whole lot smarter than following him down that hole.

Damien started down the ladder but stopped just as his foot touched the first rung. Rain dripped down his face as he looked up at Jason. "I get the feeling you don't trust me very much yet."

"No shit."

Damien smiled and stepped back off the ladder. He unzipped the front zipper of his jumpsuit and reached a hand inside. Then he pulled out a gun.

Jason's heart skipped a beat, and his muscles tensed. Before he had the chance to react, Damien flipped the gun around and extended it to him grip first. "Take it."

"What for?" Jason asked. But he accepted the offer anyway as soon as the words left his mouth. A sense of security came over him the instant his fingers wrapped around the ergonomic grip. Even though he'd always preferred a knife when killing for fun, holding a gun again felt good in a way Jason hadn't expected.

"Just hold onto it. Or go ahead and shoot me with it if you want. I'll just pop right back up. That's the thing, you see: you and I can't really hurt each other. So, if it makes you feel better to be the one holding the gun, be my guest."

Jason rotated his wrist to examine the pistol. He was no firearm expert, but it didn't look like any handgun he'd seen before. It was too sleek and smooth, like it was made from a single, flawless piece of material. But the trigger and barrel were in the right place, and that was all that mattered. Jason raised the gun and pointed it at Damien's head.

Damien's eyes widened at first, then his thin lips spread into a grin. "Alright then. I didn't think you'd actually do it, but—"

Jason pulled the trigger. It surprised him when the gun barked and sprang back against his palm; he'd half expected it to be a prop, or at least unloaded. But a real bullet left the barrel and tore through Damien's skull just below his left eye. Jason watched him drop like a ragdoll, then watched the blood begin to pool around his head.

"Well, I'll be damned," he said, giving the strange gun another once over. Then he looked down the sights again and fired four more quick rounds into Damien's scrawny body.

Maybe that'd make him stay down a while longer. Jason wasn't sure if that's how it worked, but he needed to act quickly either way. He tucked the gun into his waistband, then pried the flashlight from Damien's lifeless fingers before lowering himself into the bunker's entrance.

He shined the light down the hole once his boots were planted firmly on the ladder and saw a concrete floor some nine or ten feet down. The ladder groaned, and he wondered if its welds would hold; he must have weighed at least a hundred pounds more than the man it was used to supporting. But it got him to the bottom. Once his feet were on solid ground again, Jason took a look around.

The space was small, roughly circular, and bare, with three tunnels leading out of it—one on either side and one straight ahead. Jason swept his light across each one, unsure which one to follow. They all looked the same; just dark holes reinforced with wooden beams. Trusting his gut, he chose the tunnel straight ahead.

It wasn't as wide as it had looked from across the room. Jason had to bend a little to fit inside. He was relieved it didn't take long to make it to the tunnel's end. After about twenty feet and a sharp right turn, it emptied into a room with a higher ceiling. Jason stepped inside and shined the light around.

There was a cot at the far end of the room and a wooden table next to it. A desk sat across from it, pressed against the dirt wall and covered with a scattering of papers. Jason picked one of them up and held it up to the light. Diagrams and equations lined the ruled paper from top to bottom. Row after row of mathematical symbols Jason might have glimpsed before on a chalkboard in some movie but certainly none that he recognized. He set the paper back down in the same spot he'd found it.

There didn't seem to be much else of interest in the room. No food either, which is what he was searching for as much as anything. He gave the cot a cursory inspection and checked underneath it. Then he ducked back through the tunnel and left the room.

When he made it back to the small room where the three tunnels met, Jason shined his light up the ladder, just to make sure

Damien wasn't climbing down. He hesitated for a second, then chose the tunnel on the right.

This one went on for a little longer than the first one. Eventually, Jason came to a thick plastic curtain that hung from the tunnel's ceiling. It might have been semi-translucent at one point in time, but the layer of dust on the plastic made it impossible to see through. Jason lifted the corner of the curtain and slipped past it.

There was another bed in this room, but this one looked different. It was right in the center of the room, and there were metal rails attached to its sides. Machines that Jason didn't recognize were all around it, each one beeping and flashing and whirring. He looked for a generator powering them but didn't see one. There weren't any wires connecting the machines to an outlet either, though there were plenty connecting them to the bed.

They looked strange—too smooth and uniform just like the handgun in his waistband. One in particular caught his eye. It was shaped like a tulip or a vase, with a broad, round base that narrowed to an opening about the size of a basketball rim. Light shone from within the opening, an odd yellow-green glow that reminded Jason of what radioactive uranium looked like in comics and cartoons. There was an assortment of buttons along the machine's base, but Jason didn't dare press any of them. Even standing next to the thing made his hairs stiffen.

"I see you've found my lab."

Jason whirled around to see Damien stepping through the curtain. He kept the flashlight on him with one hand and reached for the gun with the other.

"Lights on," Damien said. There was a clicking noise, then a row of bulbs in the ceiling that Jason hadn't noticed before came on, flooding the room with white light. Jason squinted a little, then raised the gun and pointed it at Damien.

"Let's not waste anymore of our time," Damien said. "Gun deactivate."

Jason felt something shift inside the gun, like a spring releasing or a pin dropping. He pulled the trigger anyway, but it offered no resistance, as if the curve of metal was just hanging there in the trigger guard no longer connected to anything. The gun didn't even click.

Jason flipped it over to hold it like a club. Damien lifted his hands. "Easy there, big man. Let's just cool off a bit, alright?"

"Stay where you are."

Damien nodded. "All I want to do is talk."

"Fine. Start by telling me who the hell you are."

"I told you already. Dr. Damien Winters."

"The Scientist," Jason said, his tone laced with accusation. *It's The Scientist that makes my hairs stand on end,* he remembered Benjamin saying. *Something's just not right about that one.*

Damien smiled a little. "Well...that's what that old shithead Benjamin Parker thinks."

"What do you mean that's what he thinks?"

"Do you mind if I sit down?" Damien gestured toward a row of crates against the wall near where he stood. "My legs aren't what they used to be. Used to run track back in the day, you know?"

"Go on," Jason said. "But answer my question."

Damien plopped down on one of the crates and sighed. In the light, he looked even older than Jason had first guessed. Spiky white hair thinly covered his yellowing scalp, and his eyes were surrounded by wrinkles.

"I arrived here twelve years, two months, and thirteen days ago. The year was 2081 when I found this place...or when it found me, I should say. I lived in that house with Benjamin for the first four years. Then I got sick of him and left. But first, just to make sure he didn't come looking for me...because I might have stolen some supplies from him before I left, you see...I convinced him that I'd decided to turn. And that, my friend, is the answer to your question."

"How did you..." Jason started, then he latched on to something else. "Wait, what do you mean *decided* to turn?"

Damien watched him for a beat, then grinned. It was the first time Jason had seen him show his teeth; they looked too white and perfect to be natural. "He's still got you fooled, doesn't he?"

Jason didn't like the look of that grin. If he wasn't so curious to hear more, he might have wiped it off the scrawny man's face. "You better start making some sense if you know what's good for you."

Damien never stopped grinning. "I'm going to take a wild swing here and guess that Benjamin told you the people who arrive on this farm just randomly turned into those creatures out there...*the Avengers,* to borrow his quirky little term...and that there was no cause or explanation for it. Is that right?"

"Yeah," Jason said. "What of it?"

"He told me the same thing." Damien's eyes were gleaming now, and he practically hissed the next part. He almost looked the part, too—like a snake coiled up on the crate. "*But it's a lie.*"

"How's it happen then?"

"Like I said, you choose it."

"How?"

"Hmm. I'm not *exactly* sure. But I do know the first step. Step number one is stepping down a well."

"A well?"

"That's right. Not just any well, mind you. But if you go down Benjamin Parker's well, you'll end up somewhere else. Then you come out...*something else.*"

"Why would he lie about it?" Jason asked.

"Think about it..." Damien started, then shifted to something else. "You know, I just realized I never got your name?"

"Jason," he said, too engrossed to even hesitate sharing this information.

"Think about it, Jason. Old Benjamin is determined to see this thing through to the end...whatever that end might be. Now, imagine for a moment that you're a fish...a geriatric, defenseless little mackerel, let's say...trapped in a swimming pool full of sharks. Wouldn't you do everything you could to make sure there weren't... *more sharks?*"

Jason did think about it for a moment. And then it clicked. "That sneaky son of a bitch."

Damien grinned again. "He's a sly one. And completely insufferable most of the time. That's why I left. I'm going to guess it's why you left, too."

"Something like that," Jason said. He didn't want to tell this man about what had happened to the house and their food. Didn't want to tip his hand just how desperate he was.

"Well, you're welcome to stay here as long as you like," Damien said. "To tell the truth, being down here by myself all these years...well, it's just about enough to drive a person mad."

There was that glint in his eyes again. As if they'd *actually* shimmered just for an instant. Jason didn't like it. The feeling it gave him was almost as bad as his hunger. Almost. "Do you have food?"

"Of course," Damien said. "How rude of me." He hopped off the crate he was sitting on and peeled open its lid. He reached inside and pulled out a silver container, holding it in front of his face to read the label before tossing it to Jason. "Salisbury steak and mashed potatoes. Or would you rather have something else?"

"Is that a joke?" Jason asked, turning the strange container over in his hands. It looked like a small, silver serving tray with a dome lid on top, except the lid was fastened on, and there was a little red button on top of it.

Damien laughed—weirdly loud, Jason thought. "No, no, just press the button and wait fifteen seconds."

Half nervous he was about to set off a bomb, Jason pressed the button. The container started to hum quietly. A short time later—fifteen seconds, apparently—it beeped, and the lid unlocked. Jason lifted it, letting a cloud of steam escape. He could hardly believe it, but there it was: a slab of steak in bubbling brown gravy and a scoop of fluffy mashed potatoes beside it.

"Where did you get this?" he asked. His mouth was already starting to water, but curiosity had to be sated first.

"I'm a resourceful man. Go on, though. Try it. I'm curious what you think." Jason started to dig in with his hands, then he saw Damien produce a fork from somewhere. "Shall I hand it to you, or would you rather I toss it over, too?"

"Toss it."

Jason caught the fork with one hand. It crossed his mind then that maybe he shouldn't eat this man's food. There was no telling what he could have put in it. But the cramping in his stomach wasn't having it, and when the steam coming off the gravy hit his nose, he lost all resolve.

The first bite tasted heavenly. It wasn't until the third and fourth that he noticed the odd aftertaste. Something a bit like plastic or chewing gum that's lost its flavor.

"Why's it taste funny?" he asked, fixing his host in an accusatory glare.

Damien lifted his hands. "Nothing nefarious, I promise. It's only because of how it was prepared."

"Yeah? How's that?"

"You see that contraption right there?" He pointed to one of the machines in the corner. It was about the size and shape of an oven, and it was one of the few not connected to the peculiar bed at the center of the room. "That is a printer. But not an ordinary printer, no. That one can print...well, practically anything, actually. Even food."

"Where'd you get all this?" Jason asked.

There it was again; that grin Jason couldn't stand. It looked so irritating for a man with such perfect teeth and beady eyes to grin so wildly at every question he asked. And had he seen those eyes flash again? Maybe it was just the way they caught the fluorescent light, but this was the second time now that he'd noticed it.

"That's quite the story, you know," Damien said. "Might be a bit hard for you to follow, I'd fear. How familiar are you with the quantum field model of consciousness?"

Jason took a deep breath in and let it out slowly. He was getting tired of this strange little man. And now that he had some energy in him thanks to the food, every muscle itched to do something about it.

"Hmm, yes, that's what I assumed," Damien went on. "Don't feel bad, though. Why, I don't think the woman who discovered it was even born yet in the time you come from."

"Tell me what's going on here," Jason said. "In plain fucking English."

"If you'll wait just about..." Damien glanced at one of the machines near the bed then down at the digital watch on his wrist. "Two minutes and forty-six seconds, I can *show you*."

There was no mistaking it this time; Jason saw his eyes light up. Like someone had passed a light behind them, just for an instant. "What was that?"

"Hmm?"

"Your eyes. Why'd they do that?"

"Do what?"

Jason clenched his fists hard enough to turn his knuckles white. He'd had more than he could take. Bashing the guy's skull, then taking off with as many of those self-heating food trays as he could carry seemed like the best course of action.

"I'd wait just a minute if I were you, Jason," Damien said. Then he glanced at his watch again. "A minute and fifty-two seconds, to be precise."

"I don't like waiting," Jason said, stretching his shoulders. After the day he'd had, smearing this funny little man all over the walls was going to be a real treat.

"Oh, but I bet you don't like The Flip very much either, do you?" Jason ignored this and took a step toward him. "Because ninety seconds from now," Damien continued, hurrying to get the words out now that Jason was approaching, "that's what's going to happen."

Jason grabbed the man by his pencil neck. It was so thin he could just about wrap his whole hand around it. He pinned him against the wall and squeezed until Damien's beady eyes began to bulge.

"It's...too...late..." Damien said, struggling to speak as the color of his face darkened from red to blue.

A few more seconds of strangulation is probably all it would have taken. But Jason couldn't wait that long. For all the good it would do, he wanted this man dead as soon as possible. With one hand still pinning Damien to the wall, he pulled the useless (*mostly* useless) handgun from his waistband and lined up the man's eye socket like a nail he was about to hammer.

Right before he could start his swing, Jason felt the floor shift beneath him. He staggered a little, just managing to keep his grip on Damien's neck from slipping. The lights in the room flickered, and he heard the familiar sound of metal grinding in his ears.

"Ding, ding, ding!" Damien shouted. "There she blows!"

Jason's breath hitched when he saw the man's eyes. Save for the thin threads of bloodshot red, they were solid white, each one shining with a pale, artificial glow. Like there were bulbs buried within them. Jason growled and struck him on the side of the head with the gun.

It should have cracked his skull like a coconut shell. Jason had put every ounce of fear-fueled strength behind the swing. But when the butt of the pistol hit the man's temple, it felt like striking solid steel. Jason winced at the pain in his wrist as the vibrations from the impact traveled down his arm.

Damien flashed those perfect teeth again. Except there was something different about them now. It took a moment for it to register: each one was now sharpened to a needle point.

With blinding speed, Damien...*The Scientist*...grabbed hold of the arm still clutching his throat and squeezed impossibly hard. Jason heard the bone in his wrist snap at the same instant that he felt it.

"*My turn...*" The Scientist said, his voice airy and echoing unnaturally.

So fast Jason didn't have time to raise his arm and block it, the monster smashed a fist into his chin. The lights went out immediately, and Jason crumpled like a puppet with cut strings.

CHAPTER EIGHTEEN

Lying on the ground with his eyes closed, drifting just beyond the precipice of sleep, Benjamin sensed The Flip starting. The way the air turned frigid and gravity seemed to shift were signals he'd become highly attuned to, and it woke him immediately. But even as awareness sparked and fear clutched his insides with ice-cold fingers, he didn't have the energy to run. He didn't even have the energy to stand up.

Instead, he just raised his head and stared down the road. Already, he could see someone walking down it. They left a trail of flames with every step, the light from which dimly illuminated their tall, thin frame. Just enough to leave no doubt who it was.

It was The Priestess. Come to make her offering once more.

The thought of the altar's fire gave Benjamin motivation, but a wave of vertigo hit him as soon as he rose to his knees and flattened him back down to the earth. With his cheek against the ashy soil, he watched through one eye as The Priestess approached.

Her flowing robe and the exposed skin of her face and arms were both black as coal, making it impossible to tell in the darkness where one ended and the other began. But Benjamin had seen that face enough times for his mind to easily fill in the blanks. Her lips were shredded, and her nose was burned away. The rows of her exposed teeth and the jeweled amulet dangling between her burned breasts both glowed in the firelight. Cracks in the skin traced jagged lines across her singed-bald scalp, oozing blood and pale plasma. Tendrils of smoke still rose from her body as though she'd stepped from the flames just seconds ago.

"Ahmok'thar thaldor zandr'aha!!"

Benjamin had no idea what the ancient words meant, but the shrill sound of her screaming them still felt like needles in his ears. Whatever they meant, he'd heard them many times before. And he knew well what followed them.

By the time he was able to rise—first to his knees then onto wobbly feet—The Priestess was already on him. Not so close that she could reach out her charred hands and grab him, but close enough for him to see her eyes. And that was all it took.

Benjamin tried to look away, but it was too late. The sight of them had already frozen every muscle in his body. He watched with no choice but to do so as The Priestess's large, misshapen pupils began to shift and swirl. Vortexes spun to life in the inky pools, and it felt as though they pulled him straight into them.

"Ryn'varis!"

Benjamin didn't need to understand the command to obey it. His limbs responded anyway. After all that effort to get to his feet, he dropped back down to his knees.

Helpless to resist a body he no longer controlled, he stretched out his arms and bowed his head. The Priestess stood over him. Benjamin could smell her scorched flesh like meat on a spit-roast.

"Ahmok'thar gelgish!"

The monster's scream pierced his ears and forced his mind to her will. He rose again on legs that were as sturdy as ever now that his weak mind wasn't the one commanding them. The Priestess reached out a blackened, shriveled hand from beneath the singed tatters of her shawl. Without a word, Benjamin took hold of it and let her lead him into the darkness.

Hagar's Transgression

As darkness descended over the sands of Canaan, Hagar of Tyre sat on the floor of Kadesh's Temple and studied the pile of entrails before her. They'd been pulled from the belly of a lamb sacrificed at daybreak in homage to Dagon, the god of agriculture and fertility. Now, it was Hagar's job to interpret whether the deity was pleased with their offering.

To her gifted eyes, the tapestry of organs and blood-slicked intestines told a story. Staring into them for hours, Hagar had watched that story play out in her mind's eye. It had been a vision as vivid and gripping as any she'd ever experienced. She felt breathless by the end of it, and her nude body dripped with sweat.

The gods were angry. Furious at all of Canaan for the people's lack of devotion. Hagar had seen fields shriveled and dying, baking in the sun while the cracked earth cried out to the skies for water. She'd seen flies swarming the carcasses of man and beast; dead oxen scattered across pastures, dead men, women, and children littering the cobblestone streets of Tyre.

Six years of drought is what the gods threatened. A famine that would drive mothers to consume their own daughters, fathers to consume their own sons. If the gods' anger was not soothed, all of Canaan would suffer.

Still staring at the entrails in the flickering torchlight, Hagar considered what must be done. The gods demanded sacrifice. Baal demanded sacrifice. It was he most of all that the people had angered, the god of rain and storms who would not let loose his waters again until his thirst for their blood was quenched.

Under the priesthood's directive, the city of Tyre had already offered four infants at Baal's altar so far this season in preparation for the harvest. But it wasn't enough. So loudly it made Hagar's head throb, Baal cried out for more.

Only an offering of the most precious blood would satisfy him. And Hagar already knew what the offering must be.

Eight days ago, Lilith, daughter of Gideon, had given birth to her firstborn child. A healthy male-child to be called Ephraim, his father had declared at the birthing. Lilith (and, to a lesser extent, her husband Hezekiah as well) was of noble blood. For this reason, Hagar had been present at the birthing. And from the moment she watched that squalling babe slide from his mother's womb, Hagar had thought of him day and night.

There was something extraordinary about the child. Though he came into the world just like any other—wailing and unclean—Hagar had sensed it the moment she laid eyes on him. Right there in the birthing chamber, surrounded by almost every noblewoman in Tyre, she'd been struck by a vision. She'd seen the future the child was to have. She'd watched in fear and awe as the grandeur of all he would become played out before her.

Ephraim, son of Hezekiah, was to be her replacement. And not just hers, but every person of power in Canaan. He was to become a god-king, leading the people out of destitution and into an age of splendor. The mark he'd leave on the world would persist until the end of days.

Hagar's blood boiled at the thought of it. Already an old woman, she would never see this age of splendor. Only the upheaval and suffering that always precedes such times. All that she had devoted her life to, all that she believed in, would be undone. The old ways left behind. The old gods forgotten.

From the clouds where he resided, Hagar could hear Baal's rageful cries. The child's ascension could not be allowed. His blood was the only sacrifice that would calm the storm god's wrath.

It would be precarious, demanding the sacrifice of a highborn babe. Most of Tyre's offerings were sourced from the peoples the mighty Canaanite army conquered. In those rare cases where outside blood was unavailable, infants were taken from the peasants—usually those who had done something to fall out of the priesthood's good graces. But offering a child of nobility? No one had dared propose it before.

It was just as likely that *she'd* be the one who ended up on the pyre for merely suggesting it. But Hagar had no choice. The gods wanted this child dead. And though her own will mattered not, she wanted it, too.

She would need the full support of the priesthood to pull it off. Probably a decree from King Hiram as well, which meant convincing Shem—the King's personal priest-healer and Hagar's only connection in the palace—to whisper the notion in his ear. But were these not minor obstacles for someone like her? A woman so fierce and politically savvy she'd risen to the highest ranks of the priesthood in a society that held little regard for her sex.

Floating on a wave of sudden determination, Hagar rose and donned her finest robe: a flowing, raven-black garment interwoven with threads of gold. High Priest Abdi-Heba was the first man she needed to speak with. If he could be convinced, the entire priesthood would fall in line. One whisper of the vision she'd seen—a vision where his position as the highest religious leader in all of Tyre was taken from him—was likely all that would be required.

As she hastened down the stone halls of Kadesh's Temple, Hagar set her mind to the next challenge: Shem. Convincing him to convince the King would not be nearly as easy. Her relationship with King Hiram's priest-healer was long-standing but never all that close. His work kept him in the palace, and hers in the temple. What's more, Shem the Healer was known to be a stubborn man. A dangerous one, too: there were rumors he had used his influence to send more than a few of his personal and political enemies to the executioner's block.

A scroll from High Priest Abdi-Heba once he was fully won to the cause would be a good start. But what she really needed was to make the Healer's notorious wrath work in her favor. To turn him against Lilith and Hezekiah so that he'd send their child to flames with a smile. That would take some doing, but Hagar could already feel a plan starting to come together in her axe-sharp mind, materializing before her inner eye just like a vision from the gods.

When she made it to the temple's exit and stepped out into the cool night air, Hagar stopped at the edge of the stone steps. A shiver moved through her body, and a strange epiphany struck her. This would be her last chance to reconsider. Once Abdi-Heba was involved, everything that happened next would be largely out of her control.

She was struck by a paralyzing sensation then: the feeling she was about to make a grave mistake. Hagar would have ignored it, was on the verge of brushing it aside and proceeding to Abdi-Heba's dwelling. Then the world began to spin.

Her balance failed her, and she dropped to her hands and knees. The rows of torches outside the temple's entrance were all snuffed out at once like smothered candles, and Hagar was plunged into darkness.

A vision overtook her—the strange world of it materializing before her eyes like the fabric of a vivid dream. She was standing in the middle of a road, flanked on either side by tall, odd-looking plants. Hagar had never seen any plants like them before. Fruits sheathed in leaves lined their segmented stalks. On some of them, Hagar glimpsed bright yellow kernels peeking through the leaves.

There was a building ahead, at the end of the road: it, too, unlike any she had ever laid eyes on. She could make no sense of its architecture. The angles of it were unusual. The materials looked foreign and strange.

She started walking down the road. Yet the very first step she took, the vision changed. She felt her stomach drop, like the sensation of falling, and the sun darkened. She watched it blacken in the sky as if someone had tipped a pot of ink onto it.

The fields of strange stalks on either side of the road darkened, too. Shadows swooped in to obscure the narrow spaces between the rows. Then, just as Hagar noticed the sudden frost in the previously muggy air, something moved within them.

She heard the stalks rustling at the same time she saw them move. A heartbeat later, she heard more rustling behind her, and she whirled around to see something advancing toward her from that direction, too. Hagar watched it emerge from the stalks. A demon in the flesh.

She barely had time to take in its rotting face and strange, frilly clothing before a second demon exploded from the dark leaves. This one had limbs made of branches and a face made of cloth, and it held some manner of three-pronged weapon in its clutches.

Two more stepped out from the fields and joined the rest, encircling her like a wall of nightmares. Terror rose from her chest and left her mouth as a shrill scream. Then the demons descended on her.

Hagar felt them rip her apart before the vision ended. Felt every nail digging into her skin. Felt every joint and ligament separating. When she opened her eyes to see the familiar sky over Tyre instead of their monstrous faces leering down, she bolted up and drew a violent breath.

The agony faded at once. But the memory of it still seared in her brain like a coal far from cooling. What had it meant? Hagar had no idea. Some visions took time to interpret, but this had been like no vision she'd ever experienced before. It felt like an assault from the underworld, not a message from the gods.

It was the child's doing, she decided. Never mind that it didn't feel true. That voice whispering in the depths of her soul, the one that cried out against her rapidly hardening heart, was not one to be heeded. Ephraim, son of Hezekiah, was a demon—just like those that had torn her asunder.

If it was the last thing she accomplished as a priestess of Tyre, she would see him burn on Baal's altar.

Ephraim's Mission

Too young to plead and protest, squall was all the babe could do. He'd been placed into a pair of outstretched hands, but not those of his mother or nursemaid. These hands were large enough to swallow his tiny body. Baal's hands—their polished, bronze surface ice cold against the child's bare skin.

Soon enough, they would warm.

A member of the priesthood, his face painted with white streaks and his body adorned with furs and feathers, approached the altar with a torch in his hand. A pyre of dry branches had been stacked beneath Baal's outstretched arms, the top of it almost grazing the back of the hands that coddled Ephraim, son of Hezekiah.

From within the crowd gathered around, their faces glowing in the firelight, High Priest Abdi-Heba and the priestess Hagar of Tyre watched on.

The bone-dry branches caught as soon as the torch touched them. Flames climbed the pyre and began licking at the bronze. A few breathless moments passed. Then the child started to scream.

Ephraim had no concept of what was happening to him. No understanding that he was about to die. Not even the great purpose he'd been sent for had dawned on him yet. The pain and the longing for his mother to take it away were all that he knew.

Those who watched—even the few who turned their eyes in shame—had no true concept of what they witnessed either. Only the priestess Hagar knew the truth: that they were murdering their messiah.

The men and women in the crowd might have known nothing of the future going up in flames before them. The future their descendants could have had. But a few of them—those more in tune with the invisible worlds all around them—could sense, on some deep level, the great tragedy taking place. Two such onlookers, a man named Yassib and his sister, Pelaya, turned and staggered away with tears in their eyes.

When the babe at last stopped writhing against the red-hot bronze, the entire crowd of people, most of whom had witnessed many such offerings before, exhaled a collective sigh of relief. Little by little, they dispersed into the night. Some returned to their dwellings and laid down their heads, though for many, sleep did not come easily. Some wandered aimlessly through the streets of Tyre. A few went straight to the temples to beg the gods for mercy.

By the time the pyre had burned to ash and the hands of the altar had cooled, only the priestess was left standing before it. She gazed upon the god she had devoted her life to serving. A heap of lifeless metal, she realized in that moment—realized too late—useless except as an instrument of slaughter.

Eventually, she turned and walked away. She knew what she was walking toward as she trudged through the moonlit sand toward distant dunes that, to her, no longer looked like such.

Had any citizen of Tyre been watching her (and none were), they would have watched her step straight out of this world and into another. There one footfall, vanished the next. Like a desert mirage blinked away.

A full-scale inquiry would be launched by the priesthood when Hagar never returned to the temple. A trail of footprints in the sand that inexplicably ended just a hundred paces outside the city walls is all they'd ever find. But there were whispers in the bathhouses and the markets and the temples of Tyre for years to come. Tales told, with wide variation, of the priestess who burned a god in the flesh. And who was wiped off the earth for her sin.

CHAPTER NINETEEN

Once more, Jason tried with all his might to snap the strange straps around his wrists, ankles, midsection, and forehead. They seemed so flimsy, like thin rubber bands. Yet even as the metal bedrails they bound him to groaned against the strain, they didn't so much as stretch.

There was a tap against a screen somewhere behind him out of view, then Jason heard The Scientist begin to speak. "*It is day 4,457. Incident 621 of the dimensional shift. Subject is male, Caucasian, six foot three, two hundred forty-seven pounds. Neural wave readings have been... interesting.*"

"What the fuck are you doing?" Jason tried again to struggle free, but it was just an impulse now; the rational part of him had already given up that hope.

His captor didn't respond. Jason heard him open a crate, then heard him messing with something: plastic ripping, snaps fastening into place, the squeak of metal against metal.

Then footsteps getting closer. Jason tried to crane his neck to see, but the tight strap across his forehead prevented it. The footsteps stopped as The Scientist's shadow fell over him. He could see him now, looming over him behind the head of the bed. Out of nowhere, a childhood memory of getting a tooth pulled in the dentist's chair struck Jason.

Above the surgical mask he now wore, The Scientist's eyes still glowed like bulbs. From this position, they looked like the overhead lights in an operating room. He held an instrument in his pale white hands. It appeared to be an ordinary pair of hair clippers, and it buzzed like one, too, when he flicked it on. Nevertheless, Jason's heart began to beat faster.

"I am now shaving the subject's hair near the occipital bone to prepare for insertion of the ARK-26A probe."

It started beating even faster when he heard this. Jason felt the clippers dig into his scalp as The Scientist worked them in a circular pattern around the base of his skull. From the corner of his eye, he could see strands of his dark locks falling to the floor.

When the clippers stopped buzzing, he felt The Scientist's bony fingers rub something sticky and cold over the shaved skin.

"Petroleum jelly has been applied, and the ARK-26A probe has been charged to 500 joules."

Jason could see it now in The Scientist's hands—the probe. It looked like a high-tech ice pick, with a wire running from its base and connecting it to one of the machines near the bed.

"You cocksucker!" Jason spat, thrashing as much as the straps would allow, which was very little. But The Scientist didn't seem to notice. He turned a dial on the probe's handle a couple of clicks, then the device dipped out of Jason's view. "I'm going to rip you apart, you fucking weirdo!"

There was pressure against the base of his skull and a pinching pain in his scalp. He could feel the metal rod sliding against bone inch by inch, but the pain inside his skull—in his *brain*—that he'd expected never came. He caught a flash of a memory from some medical drama he'd seen on TV years ago. "There aren't any pain receptors in the brain," he heard the TV doctor say. "Because if something penetrates the brain, you're already too screwed for pain signals to have any use."

The base of the probe pressed against his shaved, jelly-slicked head and stopped there—like a thumbtack pushed all the way into a wall. But even then, the pain of his torn scalp was all Jason felt, and it was manageable. He relaxed a little, letting the air out of his lungs as his tensed muscles loosened.

"Initiating the subject's first psychic jump."

There was a click and whine between his ears. And then the pain was blinding. Blinding in a literal sense, for explosions of white light washed out his vision as agony swept from his skull all the way down to the tips of his toes. After a moment that felt like a lifetime, Jason fainted.

Or so it seemed at first. But his senses returned much too quickly. Like he'd merely blinked his eyes instead of passing out. And when they came open again, he wasn't strapped to the bed anymore.

He stood in the middle of a cemetery. Rows of headstones lining the rain-sogged ground were the first thing he noticed. He noticed the group of people next. Black coats, black dresses, black umbrellas. All gathered around an open grave with a polished gray casket beside it. The plot right next to this one had a nearly identical tombstone. The small, cheap kind that sits flush with the ground. It had been filled in not too long ago, Jason could tell; the rectangle-shaped plot of earth in front of the tombstone was just now starting to sprout green grass. But from where he stood, the names carved into the stones were a blur.

"Subject was orphaned at age four. His mother passed August 9th, 1997. The father passed April 11th, 1998."

Jason lifted his eyes to where the voice seemed to be coming from, but all he saw overhead were dark skies and falling rain. He turned his attention back to the funeralgoers, intending to march right into the middle of the proceeding and demand an explanation. But then out of nowhere, that feeling like being torn apart at the molecular level surged through his body again.

When it passed, Jason fell to his knees. Instead of sinking into the muddy cemetery soil, they landed on a white tile floor. The rows of graves were replaced with rows of matching bunk beds positioned flush against cinderblock walls. Unlike the graves, all of these were empty.

"Subject was sent to Roosevelt Boys' Home on April 19th, 1998."

Once more, the voice came from nowhere. Jason gritted his teeth and clenched his fists into balls. But confusion quickly replaced his rage. He recognized this place, this room with the wooden bunk beds and navy-blue mattresses. And the name of it, too, rang a bell. *Roosevelt Boys' Home*. The sound of those three words echoed in his head and sent dread through his heart.

"Subject experienced ongoing sexual abuse there for a period of five and a half years."

The door to the room creaked open. Jason watched the ribbon of light spilling through the crack grow larger. He flexed his hands. It didn't matter if Mother Teresa walked through that door; whoever it was, he was going to tear them apart.

But when a hulking figure big enough to cover the entire doorway stepped into the room, Jason froze. He recognized the man's bulldog face and greasy, orange hair right away.

It was the Ice Cream Man, though that's not who Jason recognized him as. It was the person he'd been before he became that monster who Jason recognized. Those feelings of déjà vu he'd experienced his first encounter with Oliver Lench crystalized into clear memories, and tears of rage stung his eyes.

Oliver stepped toward him, his fat fingers working at the zipper on his pants. Jason screamed and charged him in blind fury. But before he could make it halfway across the long room, pain paralyzed him again.

Jason went sprawling forward as every muscle in his body seized. He hit the tile floor hard, then felt it transition to rocky soil a half second later.

The rumble of cars and semi-trucks filled his ears. The smell of exhaust and asphalt filled his nose. He was underneath an overpass now. When he rose on trembling legs, he recognized it. At one point, it had been the closest thing he had to a home.

"Subject left Roosevelt Boys' Home at age eighteen. He lived homeless in Birmingham, Alabama until age twenty-six. He subsequently developed addictions to methamphetamine, alcohol...various other substances."

Jason was ready for it this time. He could sense it coming. But it still didn't make the jolt of blinding agony any less intense. He did manage to keep his balance, at least. When the agony passed and his vision returned, he was still standing—this time in the bedroom of his trailer home. The last place he'd lived in before it all really went to hell. The place where Amanda Williams had died.

There was a woman on his bed. She was passed out, silent, and it took him a while to notice her. Her hands and feet were bound to the headboard and footboard—like all the women who ended up in his bed. For an instant, Jason was sure it was her, Amanda, disregarding the fact she'd never been in this position. But this woman's hair was short and brown, not long and blonde. He recognized her face but couldn't quite place her name.

"Subject began killing at age twenty-seven. His first victim...a prostitute who went by the name Candy Rose. Real name, Mariah Gonzelez."

What happened next caught Jason completely unprepared. Suddenly, without any chance to resist, he lost control of his body—as if someone else had taken hold of the wheel. He felt himself step toward the woman despite never giving his legs the command. His hand reached for his waistline and retrieved the Bowie knife Jason didn't realize was there until the moment his fingers brushed it. He watched bewildered as—in a total surprise to him—his right wrist flicked and flipped the blade up into the air, letting it rotate a few times before catching it perfectly by the handle.

He advanced toward the unconscious woman, forced along as if dozens of invisible hands guided his limbs. He climbed up onto the bed. Climbed on top of her. He watched her chest moving rhythmically up and down and felt his arm raise the knife above his head.

Suddenly, the woman's eyes shot open. Somehow, the instant they did, Jason saw through them.

He stared up and saw his own face scowling down at him, immobilized by both the ropes around his wrists and ankles and the bizarre form and functions of a body that was not his own. He watched the body that *was* his raise the Bowie knife a final inch. Then he watched himself plunge it down.

The blade sliced through the flesh of his left breast, and pain erupted in a part of him that had never existed before. The twelve stabs that came next came in a flurry. Jason felt the first few, but the rest he only heard their wet impacts from some distant place as darkness closed on him.

Just as it seemed his consciousness would mercifully slip away, a different, more familiar pain seized him. And when cognizance returned, he was standing in the middle of an all too familiar dirt road.

"Subject arrived at the psycho-spatial anomaly on July 2nd, 2024, following the murder of the extra-dimensional being known as Amanda Williams. This brings us to the present date, Day 4,457.

The house was there again, no longer cinders and ash. Jason saw Benjamin burning a pile of trash outside it, just like he'd been doing the first time Jason walked down this road.

He had no more time to look around before he was transported violently once more. Except this time, it came full circle. He was back on the bed again in The Scientist's bunker. When he struggled against them, the straps were just as tight and strong as before.

He wondered then as he stared up at the ceiling and glowing bulbs embedded in it if this, too, was...well, whatever the rest had been. A dream. Or a simulation. Every detail of the experience had been so real it was impossible to tell if it was over.

Somewhere behind him, The Scientist cackled. It sounded more like a recording of someone laughing than someone actually there in the room—hollow and distorted in a haunting way.

"Subject has just had a humorous thought. This observation is unrelated to the trial but noted for...future enjoyment."

"Get out of my head!" Jason shouted. He could still feel the metal probe buried into his skull. In a different way, he felt something else there, too—not a foreign body penetrating flesh and bone, but a foreign mind sharing the same space as his, spying on every reflection.

"Subject exhibits diminished neural activity in the hippocampus and medial temporal lobe. Note widespread evidence of neurological damage resulting in reduced cognitive functioning and severe long-term memory loss."

"No shit, Einstein!"

Even before he'd arrived on this farm, Jason had remembered enough to know there was a lot he couldn't. In fact, between the drugs and booze and brawls, he'd made sure it stayed forgotten. But now there was an intruder in his head, tweezing at all those things he'd worked so hard to bury. Tugging them to the surface like worms pulled from the dirt.

"Functioning in the temporal lobe is equally diminished. However… subject's neuropsychic output levels in this lobe are… extraordinary."

Jason didn't like the way that sounded. He squeezed his eyes shut and tried to think of nothing. If there were no thoughts in his mind, maybe there'd be nothing to intercept.

"I will now begin subject's direct interrogation."

When Jason heard him approaching, he opened his eyes again. The Scientist reached for something on the side of the bed. Jason heard a lever disengage, then felt the bed begin to rise, inclining all the way up to a vertical position until he was nose-to-nose with the monster and staring straight into his twin-moon eyes.

"*Who are you?*" The Scientist asked. His breath felt cold against Jason's face.

"Fuck you," Jason said. It wasn't like he knew how to answer the question anyway; the monster had just flayed open his mind and peeked behind every corner. What more could he tell him?

The Scientist's eyes bore into him, so bright Jason had to squint. It was like looking into a pair of spotlights. "*Where did you come from?*"

"The whorehouse where your mother works." But once more, The Scientist didn't react. Jason got the feeling that it didn't matter if he actually answered the questions. He could say whatever he wanted; it was the thoughts beneath the surface, the subconscious response, that The Scientist was interested in.

"What *are you?*"

This time, Jason kept silent. A tingling in his scalp moved down his neck and made his whole body cold. Maybe it was the glow of those eyes or the way those thin lips never moved as the warped words left them that gave him chills. Or maybe it was the probe still wedged in his skull like a tent peg in the ground.

"It can't be..."

"Can't be what, motherfucker?" No response. "Can't be what!"

When The Scientist still didn't answer, Jason spat in his face. The string of drool landed beneath his right eye and began to drip. Calmly, The Scientist wiped it away with bony fingers, then held it up in front of his face as if studying it. A thick, coal-black tongue parted his white lips, and the monster licked his fingers dry.

"I am going to perform the Seraphim Procedure on this subject. This is a deviation from the experiment's protocol but...there is a new hypothesis that must be tested."

The Scientist disappeared behind him again. The sound of buttons clicking and fans whirring filled the room, but Jason couldn't turn his head to see what was happening.

"What are you doing?" he shouted. But it was like shouting at a stone.

When The Scientist at last came back into view, he held an ominous device in his hands. It looked like some kind of electronic syringe, with a glass barrel and a harrowingly large needle at its tip, but also a strange digital display right above the plunger.

The Scientist swiped the display, turning on the screen. He pressed a few buttons—symbols Jason didn't recognize except for one that looked like a plus sign, though who's to say what it meant either. Then he noticed something moving inside the syringe's barrel.

The liquid inside the glass was sapphire blue and looked as thick as syrup. But as The Scientist fussed with the display, it began to spark. Tiny tributaries of golden light coursed through the semitranslucent substance, moving so slowly it took them a blink or two to travel from one end of the barrel to the other. They looked like miniature lightning bolts moving in slow motion, and each time one of the hair-thin arcs fizzled out, it left a momentary trail of shiny flecks in its bright blue wake.

"I am administering 11.5 CCs of Luminite nanofluid. Artificial neuron settings have been adjusted to .1 webers and +50 millivolts."

The Scientist lifted the syringe so that the needle was pointing at Jason's face. It was large enough that he could see the little hole in its tip. Jason braced himself. He was about to get jabbed, and probably in the worst place possible, too. The eye, the way things looked. But maybe the monster would drop his hand and stick the thing right into his dick instead; expecting the worst in a situation like this was the only logical thing to do.

Instead, The Scientist lifted the syringe and stuck it into the base of the probe still buried in Jason's skull. He heard the metal against metal screech of it sliding in, then the plastic squeak of the plunger depressing.

At first, he felt nothing. Slowly, a warm, tingling feeling spread through his body. Chilled to the bone from the rain and the terror, Jason almost welcomed it. The tingling heat started in his face and spread down his chest and arms. A pounding in his ears followed, then waves of vertigo that came and went rapidly. His vision—the sight of The Scientist's drum-tight face and glowing eyes just inches from his own—would fade with each wave. Not to darkness, but to a blazing white glow that washed out all else.

"Initiating artificial neurons." There was the click of bony fingers on glass just above Jason's head. And then the blaze consumed him.

Jason screamed, certain his eyes were melting in their sockets like pieces of candy on a hot sidewalk. Not because of the pain, for there wasn't any, but because staring into something so bright without melting your eyes seemed impossible.

Voices filled his ears—a million of them all screaming (singing?) at a fever pitch. In the same way it seemed the light should have liquified his eyes, it seemed his eardrums should have burst the instant this bedlam started. The noise was so loud he could feel it vibrating his teeth.

Suddenly, the light dimmed a little. Just enough for him to notice. An instant later, the voices all fell silent. Hushed simultaneously without even a ring in his ears left behind.

He could see something ahead of him now. *Someone.* The wash of light was still too bright to make out any detail, but he could see their form.

"It's time for you to remember," a single voice whispered, so soft and gentle it sounded more like a breeze in the air, with the words carried on it just barely distinguishable.

Most emotions, Jason had stopped feeling a long time ago. But every last one of them hit him then at the exact same time. It was overwhelming. Maddening. He wanted to laugh and weep and scream all at once. And he was too paralyzed by awe to do anything at all.

This synthesis of feelings, most not felt since the forgotten years of childhood, faded at the same time the light did. By the time his view changed back to that of the underground bunker and The Scientist still standing in front of him, his heart felt empty as ever again.

Empty, but surging with power.

Jason flexed his wrists and snapped the once unbreakable straps around them like they were made of brittle rubber. The ones around his feet and forehead didn't even slow him down as he took a step toward The Scientist. He'd expected to see surprise, maybe even fear, in the monster's expression. Instead, his lips stretched into a smile.

"*Yes! Yes! I* knew it."

Jason grabbed him by his neck with one hand and lifted him into the air, walking him back until he was pressed against the wall. He reached his other hand above his head and wrapped his fingers around the probe, sliding it out of his skull in one smooth motion. All the while, The Scientist continued to grin.

"Initiating subject's first psychic jump, motherfucker."

Jason thought he heard the monster start to laugh, but he didn't give him the chance. With more force than his body had ever generated, he drove the probe into The Scientist's skull and watched until those glowing eyes went dark.

Aiko's Mission

Shivering in the darkness of a cold and barren cell, Aiko Fujimoto reminisced on a dream she used to have. Reminisced in the way you might mourn a lost loved one, for this dream, too, was dead.

It had died for good the day she met Dr. Winters. But maybe it had been dying long before then. Maybe the war had killed it when it killed her family. Or maybe the man she met when she was seventeen—the one whose name she never learned but whose twisted face and rum-scented breath she'd never forget—had struck the mortal wound even before then.

If she was being honest, though, Aiko knew when her dream had truly begun to die. It had withered like a plant cut from its roots the moment she entered this broken world.

She used to scold herself for being so naïve. But how could she have understood? How could she, having known only an existence free of pain and sorrow—free of choice and consequence as well—have been prepared for all that awaited her here? It made her angry to think about it sometimes. What they'd done to her had been like sending a child to war—which happened to be just one of the many horrors she'd witnessed firsthand in her twenty-four long, long years of earthly life.

So funny and sad as well that she'd spent a hundred times a hundred the length of those years dreaming of what they'd be like. Pondering how it would feel to take on flesh and immerse in all the wonders of life.

Most of Aiko's kind (though that wasn't the name she went by when she was still with them) were perfectly content with their stations. Content to live out eternity as servants in paradise. And, if ordered to be, Aiko could have been content as well. But when the chance to go finally came, the chance to right a wrong that should never have existed and serve a purpose, in her eyes, much more meaningful, Aiko took it without hesitation.

Oh, how she regretted it now.

She knew what her mentor would say: that she should absorb the lessons of this life even though her mission had failed, so that whenever it mercifully ended, she could return with a new perspective and better suited to serve. But how could truly knowing those whom she served possibly make her want to serve them better?

The distant click of Oxford shoes on a tile floor interrupted Aiko's silent lamentations. In the total deprivation of her quiet, lightless cell, she picked up the familiar sound right away. Hearing it used to turn her blood cold. At this point, she felt practically nothing. He would kill her eventually, whether he meant to or not, and that was all Aiko hoped for now. Every time he drugged her and dragged her out of this cell just brought her closer to that day.

When the lock on her cell door turned and the light from the other side flooded in, Aiko lowered her head. There was no point in resisting. She couldn't escape. And she didn't want to even if she could. Out there, beyond these walls, she might live another seventy years. That sounded so much worse than a few more weeks or months here.

Dr. Winters didn't speak to her as he entered her cell. He rarely ever spoke outside of his recorded trials with her. What does a scientist have to say to a lab rat, after all?

Aiko felt his cold fingers brush the hair away from her neck and did everything she could not to flinch. Then she felt the needle pierce her skin.

When darkness beckoned, Aiko embraced it. Practically threw herself into its arms. For a moment, in the dreamless, drug-induced sleep, she found peace.

"It is 6:43 p.m., January 3rd, 2081. Subject has just woken. Vital signs are all good. Neural readings…normal, as it were."

Aiko wasn't sure which came first: the voice or her eyelids fluttering open. The metal table she lay strapped to was stinging cold against her skin. The bright, LED bulbs overhead hurt her eyes. But waking to these things was something Aiko had grown used to.

"I will now ask the subject a series of calibration questions."

Aiko didn't turn her head toward the voice. She knew what she'd see if she did. Dr. Winters would be sitting cross-legged in his worn-out rolling chair, watching her with one eye and watching the array of displays on his desk with the other.

"When were you born?"

"October 11th, 2056," Aiko replied. Ignoring him was no use. One way or another, he always got an answer.

"When did you come to the United States?"

"When I was nineteen. I came from Japan on a student visa. To study neurology at UCLA."

"What was the worst day of your life?"

He asked the same questions every time. This conversation between her and Dr. Winters—the only one they ever had—never changed. But, depending on her mood, there were a couple different ways Aiko would answer this question.

Sometimes she'd tell him that the worst day of her life was the day she walked into his office at UCLA and applied to be a research assistant. All she'd known of Dr. Winters at the time was that he was a pioneer of quantum consciousness theory and, more importantly, someone offering a job that sounded a lot more interesting than waiting tables at one of the few non-automated restaurants left in the city.

This time, she decided to give the answer she thought, on the whole, was probably truer. "The worst day of my life was when the People's Liberation Army dropped a kinetic rod on Tokyo. My parents, brother, and two of my cousins were killed. My best friend and her entire family, too."

This story had never fazed Dr. Winters, and it didn't now. He just skipped right on to the next item on his predictable questionnaire. "What was the best day of your life?"

The first time she'd woken on this table, probably about two years ago, she figured, answering this question had been difficult.

But now she gave the same well-practiced answer as always. As far as she knew, as far as she cared, it was true. "I was six. My parents took me to Disneyland, the one in Tokyo, for the first time. I got to take a picture with Donald Duck."

"What are you?"

Shamefully, Aiko's answer to this was just as well-practiced. There'd been a time when she used to make him drag it out of her. She liked to think she'd been brave for enduring so much, holding out for so long, before he finally broke her. But she'd felt like such a coward ever since.

"I am an angel. A being not of this world."

It was the second phrasing that Dr. Winters preferred. An "extra-dimensional consciousness" was actually the term he liked most.

"What is your purpose here?"

With this question came its own flavor of shame. Aiko sighed and recounted her failure. "My mission was to locate an anomalous realm created when the angel known as Eden Donnovan was killed, to visit it in the flesh, and to help those trapped there."

It was a mission she could have completed at any point in the twenty-two years before she became Damien Winters' subject. That was the part that hurt worst of all. She'd been so determined to do more good with her life—to go above and beyond her calling—that she'd waited too long.

"Calibration successful. Neural readings remain stable. Ready to initiate psychic jump sequence number forty-seven."

Now came the brutal part. The part certain to kill her eventually. Aiko wondered if this would be the time that did it. Sadly, she didn't think so. She still felt too strong.

She kept her eyes closed and tried to calm her racing heart while Dr. Winters fussed about around her, double-checking the electrode pads stuck to her skin and the IV in her arm. In a way, this final check, the dread of waiting for the axe to drop, was always the worst part. The few minutes that passed before Dr. Winters returned to the monitor at his desk felt like hours.

A machine beside her started to whir. Instead of its chilling growl, Aiko tried to imagine the sound of her mother singing. Every night she used to sing when Aiko was a child. It had always been the last sound Aiko heard before falling asleep. Someday—someday soon, she hoped—it would be the last sound she heard in this world.

With the push of a button, a tidal wave of pain swept through her, contracting her muscles and sucking the breath from her lungs. On her own accord, she wouldn't have been able to think of anything except the pain. But in these moments, her mind wasn't really hers to control anymore.

Dr. Winters, the man who had unlocked more secrets of the human consciousness than any person in history, sent hers hurtling through planes of existence the body couldn't travel. Back to the place she'd come from.

Just for a moment, she glimpsed it again. The transcendent, golden light. The impossible geometries of a realm unbound by physical constraints. The blissful, euphoric feeling that was just as much a characteristic of this place as anything else.

It was gone again in a heartbeat. Just a lightning flash of recollection—brilliant but fleeting. Then the pain slowly subsided. The sound of machines humming filled her ears again, and the view of the ceiling and overhead lights in Dr. Winters' laboratory came back into focus.

"Psychic jump sequence number forty-seven successful," she heard him say. "Transient event lasted 1.63 seconds, .11 seconds longer than the median time."

Aiko fought to catch her breath, but her lungs didn't want to do their job. She shook violently from head to toe, every muscle spasming. She would have been sick if there'd been anything on her stomach, but Dr. Winters was careful not to feed her on the days he ran this experiment.

"Note an interesting observation in quadrant E6 of the psychophysical dimension. Some kind of...obelisk. Large, pure white...flowing, in a way."

Aiko's breaths were starting to steady. Her body had stopped convulsing. "That's all..." She took one more shuddering breath and started again. "That's all you're ever going to see of it, you know. Just a glimpse. A glimpse on a screen."

Dr. Winters didn't respond, but with her senses still heightened, she could feel him seething. Admit it or not, he knew it was true. Places like the one she came from—the one he longed so badly to understand—were not meant for men like him. He must have felt it in his shriveled heart with every fleeting glance he stole.

"Preparing to initiate psychic jump sequence number forty-eight." Dr. Winters said. The cold, professional tone he always adopted when recording these sessions couldn't hide his anger.

Aiko let her eyes close again. Even as her heart thrummed, her body dreading another round, a smile touched her lips. It would be over soon, she thought as her mother sang *Toryanse* and *Neko Funjatta,* both songs core memories from the last time she was happy. It would all be over soon.

Damien's Transgression

For as long as he could remember, Dr. Damien Winters had been a man who trusted only that which could be observed. Proven beyond reproach using methods meticulous and unbiased. And what could be more undeniable than seeing with one's own eyes?

Yet staring down a road all too familiar, he thought his eyes must be deceiving him. Maybe it was a dream, or a hallucination of sorts. That seemed plausible. More plausible than accepting it as reality, at least.

But then there was the wind against his face and the subtle scent of ripe corn it carried—a strong confirmation of the story his eyes told. And when he knelt and ran his fingers through the dust, it felt warm and gritty.

Fear gripped him then, but so, too, did a sense of awe. Here was a reality of pure psychic origin, made manifest by mind rather than matter. Yet every bit as real.

He thought of the implications merely knowing such a thing was possible would have on the field of consciousness research.

The realization that the conscious mind isn't just an instrument for perceiving reality but an engine that shapes it.

Such a shame he'd never be able to share these discoveries.

He knew what this place was. He'd seen it many times before. Never in the flesh, like he saw it now, but in virtual renderings derived from the mind of Aiko Fujimoto. When he thought of her, he thought next of how she'd looked lying lifeless on his table with clouds in her unblinking eyes. It tore at his heart.

He had loved her. Not in a romantic way; Dr. Winters had never loved anyone that way. But he had loved her in the way da Vinci must have loved the Mona Lisa, or Michelangelo the Sistine Chapel. She had been his masterpiece. Without question the single greatest discovery in the history of humankind. Perhaps, if he'd realized it sooner, he might have done things differently.

No turning back now, though. Turning back wasn't possible on this road. Pressing forward, unearthing the secrets of this place, learning, if possible, how to control it—escape it, maybe, he could dare to hope—that was his only option now.

Horrors unthinkable awaited him at the end of this road. But so did a man Dr. Winters was quite keen to speak with. Benjamin Parker was his name. Aiko had told him all about the man…though told perhaps wasn't the best word. *Shown him* was closer.

When Dr. Winters made it about halfway to the farmhouse that stood at the end of the road, he saw its front door swing open. Benjamin Parker stepped out wearing nothing but a pair of briefs and holding an old, wooden stock rifle in the crook of his arm. Dr. Winters waved at him.

Of all the things to dread here—and there were many—meeting this man was the one thing Dr. Winters looked forward to. After all, if there was anyone who knew the secrets of this place, it was the man responsible for creating it.

CHAPTER TWENTY

Benjamin woke with a gasp. A gust of cold wind cut through his clothing, chilling him deeply and prickling his skin into goosebumps. Yet for a moment before the feeling passed, it felt like he was still on fire.

Lying on the barren, ruined ground outside where his house used to stand, he stared up at the winking stars. The same stars had watched his skin and flesh melt away in Baal's searing hands what seemed like just seconds ago.

His body shook, and tears poured out of his eyes. He had no inclination to rise from his fetal position on the ground. Where would he go if he did? Staggering into the wilderness, like Jason had done? They'd find him there just as easily as they'd find him lying here.

There was no point in trying, Benjamin decided. No point in running, that was a given, but no point in trying to make the best of things anymore either. You can't squeeze blood from a stone, he remembered his grandmother saying in some other lifetime. Some other world. And you can't squeeze goodness from a place where there is none.

Better to lie in the dirt and wait to die, over and over again.

Maybe, he thought, that's what she'd wanted from him all along. Resignation. That was only wishful thinking, though. He already knew what she required.

He pictured her face, as best he could remember it, even though it hurt to do so. Thinking about her was always such a noxious cocktail of emotions. Resentment mostly—hatred even—but there were lingerings of the things he used to feel about her, too: fascination and enchantment. Adoration. Love.

What he'd done to her was wrong. Unforgivable, maybe. Was what she'd done to him any better, though? He had killed her once. She had killed him countless times and counting.

"What do you want from me!" Benjamin screamed into the night. Screamed up at the stars.

The stars whispered their reply: an answer Benjamin had heard already too many times before. But he couldn't do it. It would be better to stay here another thousand years than do what she asked.

"This is your fault, too," he said. He knew in his soul that she was listening. "What I did to you was wrong, but you made me do it. You could have given me anything. *Anything*! You hear me? And you denied me! You spat in my face and told me you'd rather die!"

A strong gust of wind stirred the dust and ash where he lay. It whipped at his hair and whined through the trees beyond his farm.

And did the soft yet clear voice that spoke to him come from it? Or maybe from the stars again.

I gave you everything, Ben. Just not what you wanted.

Benjamin pressed his face into the dirt and wailed. Hearing her voice—those words—hurt worse than any whip or blade or altar fire. They hurt because of all the memories they evoked.

They hurt because they were true.

Eden's Mission

For some conditions, there simply is no cure. Having devoted her entire earthly life to the purpose of curing just a single disease, Eden Donnovan knew how challenging it could be.

But some conditions made curing actual diseases like cancer and polio look easy in comparison. At least to a scientist like her. Take love, for instance. Maybe it was a condition most people had no desire to cure, but Eden Donnovan was not most people.

In fact, getting to the point where she even considered herself a person at all should have been her first warning sign. The first shot across the bow that she was starting down a risky path. How easy it was to forget all that had come before this life now that she was here in human flesh. Just thirty-four years in this world and already the near-infinite span preceding them hardly felt real anymore. It felt more like the memory of a dream she'd once had.

It was precisely that kind of thinking that was dangerous. Dangerous to her mission. Dangerous to the entire world if she let it go far enough. Beings like her, angels sent to earth, had only their purpose to keep them grounded. A rogue angel…a *fallen angel*...could be a terrifying force of destruction. It had happened before.

Come whatever, her mission had to come first. If it meant working herself to the bone every hour of her life, so be it. If it meant telling that young man she'd met—the one who sent her heart galloping every time he crossed her mind—that she couldn't see him anymore...well, so be that, too.

It wasn't that angels sent to earth were forbidden to fall in love. All things were allowed as long as the mission came first. But the mission *had* to come first. Always. Without compromise. And the more an angel allowed themselves to indulge in all the world's pleasures, the more difficult that became.

Take right now, for instance. She should have been focused on preparing the latest batch of cell samples. The lab was waiting on her. The entire human race was waiting on her, whether they knew it or not. And instead, here she was, daydreaming about a boy.

Humming softly to clear her thoughts, to drown out the distracting ones, Eden set her focus on her work. Its importance could not be overstated. The year was 1953. Researchers at the Johns Hopkins School of Medicine were already laboring diligently to discover a cure for cancer. Left to their own devices, it would be another century before anyone unlocked the secret. Hundreds of millions of people would die waiting. This was why Eden had been sent. To speed up the timeline.

But an angel's mission is rarely easy. It's meant to test them, more times than not, and Eden knew this was the case for the mission she'd been given. She was being considered for elevation to Heaven's Second Sphere, and how she performed here on earth would undoubtedly influence that decision.

She'd been given all the tools she needed to succeed: a brilliant mind, a privileged upbringing, a supernatural talent for medicine. But she'd not been given the answer. That, she would have to discover on her own.

The rest of the afternoon, Eden committed herself to her work. Committed herself fully, so that by the time five o'clock came around and the lab closed down for the evening, she nearly forgot about her date. Hurrying home to change and make herself presentable before he arrived to pick her up, Eden felt both thrilled and ashamed by the butterflies fluttering in her chest.

Sitting at the corner booth of Howard Johnson's, Eden was struck with the feeling that she'd already lived this moment. It was no surprise; she practically had already lived it. Several times, actually. Howard Johnson's was Benjamin Parker's favorite restaurant, at least among those he could afford to frequent. And he liked this particular booth, too. It was near the window, and she'd noticed that he liked to look out sometimes at the trail of traffic lined up along I-95. When he wasn't looking at her, that is.

He was looking at her now. With his elbows resting on the Formica table and his chiseled chin resting on his knuckles, he stared at her as though he saw straight through the façade. So many men she'd met were too timid to gaze for long at a beauty such as she, to set their eyes unwavering on what their heart desired, but not Benjamin. He hardly ever stopped staring. If he hadn't been so kind and charming (and handsome, that helped, too), Eden might have found it unsettling. As it was, she found it endearing.

"Tell me again," Benjamin said, "just one more time, what it is you do?"

"I'm a cancer researcher."

"No, I remember that part. But...what I guess I'm asking is, how?"

"As in, how does one research cancer?"

"Yeah."

"It depends on what you're trying to learn. The most common method is to take cancer cells and study them under a microscope to see how they grow and respond to different treatments."

"But that's not what you do, though, right?"

"Not exactly." Eden paused, trying to think of the best way to explain her work; Benjamin wasn't a dull man, quite the opposite from what she'd seen, but he lacked any higher education. He certainly lacked the depth of knowledge required to understand the human genome and her efforts to unlock its secrets. Even most of her colleagues at the university fell short there.

"Your mother and father probably both have blue eyes, right?" she finally said. Benjamin's own eyes were blue—strikingly blue—so it was a safe bet, given the trait's recessive nature.

"Yes, ma'am. Both of 'em."

"But did you know that blue eyes are a genetic mutation? They just keep getting passed down from one generation to the next, but they weren't ever supposed to exist. If it weren't for the mutation, an accident of nature, you could say, everyone's eyes would be brown."

"That's real interesting," Benjamin said, dipping a french fry in the ketchup spilled from his burger. "But what's it got to do with curing cancer?"

"Because cancer's a mutation, too. Just like blue eyes. Cancer cells are created when your DNA goes haywire. It's like starting with a faulty blueprint; you're going to end up with a faulty house. Except in this case, what you end up with are cancerous cells."

"And what you're doing is..." Benjamin waited for her to fill in the rest, utterly engrossed.

"Figuring out how to stop DNA from going haywire."

"Sounds impossible. Like something only God could do."

"Maybe it is," Eden said, though she knew that wasn't true. If it was impossible, she would not have been sent.

"I got to say, though...and I promise I'm not just buttering you up...but I think if anyone can do it, it's you."

Eden smiled a little. It felt like she blushed a little, too, and she hoped it wasn't obvious; with skin as fair as hers, hiding her abashment wasn't always easy. "Now, Mr. Parker. No need to fib. I know good and well when a man's trying to butter me up."

"No, I mean it," Benjamin said. "I know we haven't been seeing each other all that long, but...there's just something special about you, Eden Donnovan. I can't quite put my finger on it yet, but it's there."

This time, when Eden shifted in her seat, it was more than just humility making her uncomfortable. Again, it seemed like he saw right through her. Saw a glimpse of who—*what*—she really was.

And that, no matter how close she let him get, was something Benjamin could never know.

The seasons all take on new meaning when you spend the whole year falling in love. Spring of 1953 had been a time of blossoming feelings and newfound sensations. Summer a time of simmering passion and autumn a time of sweet comfort.

Now winter had arrived. Eden could feel its bite on the wind every time she stepped outside. She supposed there was no need to dread it as much as she did. Winter, after all, did bring its own delights: fires in the hearth, Christmas trees and Christmas dinners, and warm blankets big enough for two.

But the cold she felt in the air stirred in her something deeper than the chills. It was a feeling like that of a winter storm on the horizon, one that would freeze over all the warmth she'd kindled this past year. Turn it all to ice.

For his part, Benjamin seemed to look forward to the cold. It made sense, she supposed. Winter was always the least busy season for farmers, the only time of year they got to rest. And Benjamin did work so very hard.

This plot of land he'd purchased in Northeast Maryland—the 60 acres with a farmhouse near its center where she spent most of her free time lately—was not a good one. No good for farming, anyway. Rocks were the only thing that grew easily from its soil. It seemed to always get too much rain, or not enough, and Benjamin alternated continuously between digging ditches to guide the water to his crops and ditches to guide it away.

The land's poor suitability for farming was why he'd been able to purchase it so cheap. That had been three years ago, according to what he'd told her. He didn't tell her this next part himself, but Eden imagined he must have been undaunted then in the way young men just starting out on their own often are. But three hard years of toiling in unforgiving soil, and she could see his confidence starting to falter.

She wanted to help him. Day and night, she dreamed of it. Just a touch of her hand was all it would take to turn the land into a paradise, a true Garden of Eden where he could live like a king. And her his queen who wanted nothing.

In the quiet times like this when Benjamin was out doing chores and she was alone in the house, such whisperings grew so loud she could almost hear them in her ears. There was no doubt where these voices and their tempting suggestions came from; the veil separating the domains of darkness from the earthly realm was so much thinner than most realized. And listening to them—eating of the apple they offered—would mean abandoning all else.

From there, her thoughts wandered (as they quite often did) back to guilt and shame. It was because of the vulnerable position she'd put herself in by being with Benjamin that the demons had set her in their sights. She'd made herself weak. And they could smell it.

Before she could spiral too far down this funnel of self-contempt, Eden heard the back door groan open. She got up from the rocking chair where she sat and walked into the kitchen.

Benjamin stood by the door, brushing snowflakes from his blonde hair that melted against the warm hardwood almost as soon as they fell. On the kitchen counter beside him, Eden spotted a small cedar box with flecks of fresh dirt still clinging to it.

"Did you get the fence fixed?" she asked him.

Benjamin seemed to notice her looking at the box, and he picked it up and clutched it tight against his wool jacket. "Well... to tell you the truth, the fence didn't actually need fixin'. That might have been a little fib. But for a good purpose, I promise."

Eden felt her heart begin to speed up. It came to her then, without her even trying, what lay inside that box, and a dizzying wave of conflicting emotions followed on its heels.

"I buried this box when I first bought this farm," Benjamin continued. If he'd looked close enough, maybe he would have seen the storm swirling behind her emerald eyes. But he was too caught up in the waves of his own emotions, she realized, to have any chance of noticing. "I swore to myself I wouldn't dig it up again until I was certain I'd found the right girl. I'd have left it there forever before I dug it up for the wrong one."

Eden wondered if she should say something. If she should stop him now before the box and his heart were both bared open. But time kept moving faster than she could keep up. A few bewildered blinks later and Benjamin was down on one knee.

"Eden Donnovan," he said. The box's lid came open. Eden saw a glint of rainbow fire from inside. "Will you marry me and make me the happiest man in the whole wide world?"

"*Benjamin,*" she said. So many emotions bled into her voice: love and joy, fear and worry all at once. "I...I don't know what to say."

Benjamin swallowed. He'd kept his confidence this far, but now was the first sign of it faltering. "Well, Eden...there's only two options to choose from, I reckon."

Eden laughed, surprised when it slipped out unexpectedly. She took a deep breath and fixed her love in a warm yet serious gaze. "You know that if I say yes, my miss...my work still has to come first. Always. It's too important to play second fiddle to anything, Ben. Even you."

"I understand."

"There will be nights when I don't come home until it's already dark out. Weekends I have to spend at the lab. It's nothing different than the way it's been for us so far, but that's the point. It's not going to change just because we're married. It can't."

"Listen to me," he said, rising to his feet and placing his hands on her shoulders. "Listen to me real close, because I mean this, alright: I don't want to change a damn thing."

Tears began to blur Eden's eyes. "It's going to be hard sometimes, you know?"

"Not half as hard as it would be without you."

She felt like hugging him, kissing him, and sobbing all at once. It was difficult to even get the next words out with so many emotions wanting to spill out instead. "I...yes, then! My answer is yes."

A grin lit up Benjamin's face and spread to Eden's, too. She watched him fumble for a second with the ring to get it out of the box, then she let him slip it over her finger. It was sizeable—both the diamond and the band, the latter of which was so large she had to clench her fingers to keep it from slipping off. It was likely his mother's or his grandmother's ring, Eden assumed. And with a bit of twine to tighten its fit, it would suit her just fine.

She kissed Ben...*her fiancé's* lips while snow fell in perfect flakes outside the kitchen window. For a moment in time, the whole world was just as perfect.

Time doesn't always move at the same pace. As a being who once existed outside of time in a place unaffected by its march, Eden still struggled with this. It seemed like the moments you want to end always drag on forever. And the moments you want to last forever always go by in a flash.

So it had been for the wedding, and the honeymoon Ben promised her wasn't the "real honeymoon" they'd take one day (even though Eden never complained), and the three blissful months that had passed since. The only thing wrong with any of it was that it had all passed by so quickly. Like a shooting star in the sky: bright, breathtaking, but fleeting.

Something had been troubling Benjamin lately. She'd prodded gently, but he wouldn't tell her what it was. He'd always say it was a headache, or exhaustion, or the pressures a man has to bear. Maybe these things were true, but there was something else there, too. A storm brewing inside him that she could clearly sense. A few days ago, she'd given up on trying to get him to talk; the clouds would burst eventually, when they could hold their burden no more.

Tonight, lying in bed beside him, she could tell that it was close. She'd been reading by the light of their nightstand lamp for almost an hour. Benjamin had lain there staring up at the ceiling the entire time, not saying a word. She kept having to re-read the biochemistry text's dense passages, finding it hard to focus on anything but him and what thoughts were swirling behind his troubled eyes.

"Eden," he said a little while later. The sudden break of silence almost startled her. "I want to talk about something."

Eden's heartbeat quickened, but she felt relieved at the same time. Whatever was bothering him had festered long enough. It was time to pull out the arrow and let it start to heal. "I'm always willing to talk to you, Ben."

Benjamin stared at her. He was sitting up in bed now, his back against the headboard. "Are you willing to tell me the truth?"

She waited for him to elaborate, but he only watched her, waiting for an answer. "Darling, I don't know what you mean."

Though maybe she did. Maybe she'd known all along and just refused to admit it.

"You've been hiding something from me, Eden. I don't have any idea what it is. But I know you are."

She knew those words would come someday. It isn't possible to share so much of yourself with someone and expect them to never discover the parts you hide. "I'm so sorry, Ben." The words slipped out before she could consider them. She meant them deeply.

"So it's true."

"Yes."

"Tell me," he said, twisting in bed and placing his hand on her leg. Eden didn't know if it was meant to be comforting or something else. Demanding maybe. Giving her no option to leave. "Tell me what it is. I won't be angry, Eden. We all have our sins."

"No, it's...it's nothing like that."

"Alright. What is it then?"

Part of her wanted to tell him. Her secret burned inside her all the time and burned hotter than ever right now. "Ben...it's better if you don't know. Please trust me."

"No," he said after a few long moments. "That's not going to work. You need to trust me, Eden. Whatever it is, you need to trust me with the truth."

It wasn't that she didn't trust him, though; if he knew what she was, he'd never look at her the same. It would forever be different between them. Eden couldn't say how it would change things, but she knew it would. How could it possibly not?

"Listen to me," she said, quickly wiping a tear from her eye. Now was not the time to break down crying. She had one chance to make him understand. "There's something you don't know about me. There is something you can never know about me. And I'm so sorry, Ben, because I understand how unfair that is to you. But there is no other way. If you can live with that, if you can let it go and love me anyway, I'll love you back forever with all my heart. If you can't..." Eden trailed off. The rest was too painful to say.

She watched him, waiting breathlessly for his response. "Fine, Eden," he said after what felt like forever.

No more was said between them that night. But Eden knew the truth, and it broke her heart to pieces. It wasn't fine. It would never be fine again.

Benjamin's Transgression

Guiding a plow through soil that mocked his every effort, Benjamin Parker set his eyes straight ahead and pushed forward. His mule, Lankey, was the one doing all the pulling, but keeping the plow straight and the blade pressed into the earth was hard work, too. Especially in soil this rocky.

As if on cue, the blade struck a large one. Benjamin felt the impact rattle through his wrists and heard the gritty grind of steel against stone.

"Whoa!" he said and gave the reins a tug. Lankey stopped pulling. "*Damn it.*"

If the blade was ruined, he would be, too. Already two weeks behind schedule, he had to get his corn seed in the ground soon or the plants would have a shortened growing season. In earth where nothing grew easily even when he did everything right, it was the last thing he needed. The previous year's crop had only produced a fifty percent yield. Barely enough to cover what he'd spent on seed and fertilizer. If this year wasn't better, the bank was going to come knocking.

Eden's paycheck from the university helped, but it could only go so far. He'd always resented having to rely on her. Lately, he'd come to resent her for a much different, deeper reason.

It had taken three long months for her to finally break down and tell him what she'd been keeping from him. Benjamin wasn't proud of the things he did to get it out of her. The sulking and the guilt-tripping and the cold way he'd treated her. But he couldn't live without knowing.

His reaction had surprised her when she told him the truth. He supposed she'd been expecting him not to believe it, but he'd accepted it right away; believing that Eden Donnovan was an angel from Heaven was the easiest thing in the world.

Accepting it as true was one thing. Accepting everything else... well that just wasn't going to be so easy.

He had tried to understand her. Tried to see things from her perspective. But each time she denied him, the same resentment burned hotter and hotter: that she didn't love him enough to do it anyway.

"I'm dying inside, Eden," he had told her three days ago. "It's not cancer, but it's gonna kill me just as dead."

She had only stared at him with that damned sorrowful look in her eyes. The way Benjamin saw it, you couldn't really be sorry about something if you were capable of fixing it and refused.

He glanced up at the raging sun to gauge the time and figured it was about four. Eden would be coming home soon. She usually left the lab early on Fridays. Benjamin dreaded seeing her. He planned to work out here until dark—not like he had any choice either way—but then he'd have to sit at the dinner table with her, then crawl into the same bed. All while she continued to pretend it was all okay.

She probably wouldn't pretend much longer, Benjamin figured. Sooner or later, he was going to lose her, if he didn't do something about it. It hurt to think about, but not as much as the other ways she'd already hurt him.

Half an hour later, he saw her car coming up the road. Used to, on days like this, he could count on her to walk out into the field and greet him. This time, she went straight inside. Off to relax the rest of the day away, probably.

Probably not, if Benjamin was being honest; Eden worked as much as him, as much as anyone, between house chores and her job. That didn't matter, though. She still didn't understand what a man went through. The price that must be paid if he's to scratch out a living from the unforgiving dirt. The mental, physical, and spiritual burdens he has to bear.

Eden worked because she wanted to. Because life was just a *mission* to her. A brief little interlude in her existence that never had, and never would, truly matter. Well, it mattered to him. He wasn't going to suffer this life in shame and destitution just because she promised a better one awaited.

For the next four hours, Benjamin worked on prepping the south field for planting. And with every stone his plow head struck, with every root he tripped over and every bead of sweat that rolled off his brow, his anger grew. By the time he'd put the plow in the barn and Lankey back in his stable, night had settled in, and the air had cooled. But Benjamin's blood boiled hotter than ever.

"Do you still love me?" Eden asked while Benjamin sat in the chair and listened to a baseball game on the radio. It was the second game of a doubleheader between the Cubs and the Yankees, and he'd not spoken to her since the first game started.

"Yes," Benjamin said. But he'd had to think about it for a moment, and he could tell by the hurt in her eyes she'd noticed.

"I want to fix this. I...I know how you feel. And you know how I feel, and neither one of us is going to change our minds, Ben. We've been at it for months now. There has to be a way for us to move past this."

"And that's a hard hit to left field!" the radio announcer shouted, his voice flown on the airwaves all the way from Chicago. "Bolger is charging and gets it in to the cutoff man, but that's gonna score McDougald from third."

"Shit," Benjamin muttered, none too quietly.

"Ben, please." Eden stepped in front of his chair and dropped down to her knees, placing both hands on his. He glanced down at her, saw the desperation in her big green eyes, and, for just a moment, his hardened heart broke for her.

"What's left to talk about anymore, Eden?" he said. But he reached over to the end table and turned the radio down anyway. Because maybe deep down he still wanted to fix it, too.

"I want you to think about something," Eden said. "Can you do that for me?" Benjamin sighed but agreed with a nod. "Think about what it would have been like for us if I had never told you what I am."

Benjamin couldn't see where she was going with this yet, so he didn't think about anything except trying to figure that out.

"Our lives would have been just as hard," Eden went on. "But you and I would have still been happy."

"You know what would happen if a frog had wings, Eden?" Benjamin asked.

"No," Eden said, seeming prepared to be disappointed with the answer.

"It wouldn't bump its ass on the ground every time it jumped." Eden just stared at him, even though he was pretty sure she knew exactly what he meant. "Point is, 'ifs' are worthless. You did tell me. You told it to me just like this, Eden: 'Hey husband I say I love more than anything, turns out I'm an angel straight from Heaven, can you believe it? And if I wanted to, I could snap my fingers and make your miserable life a paradise. But guess what, and hold on tight because here's the punchline…I ain't gonna fucking do it.'"

"You know it's not that simple," she said, But her voice was weak, already defeated; she'd tried many times before to explain just how not simple it was.

"I know that if you want something bad enough, if you love someone bad enough, you make it happen."

It took a while for Eden to respond. Benjamin started to think they were going to leave the conversation at that. Or leave it there for now, anyway; it surely wouldn't be long before they returned to it again. But then she looked up at him, and though there were still tears pooling in her eyes and her voice was still so soft he could hardly hear her, Benjamin could sense her resolve.

"I do love you, Ben. I can't prove that to you in the way you want me to. But there are so many other ways I'm willing to spend the rest of my life proving it to you. If that's not enough, if *I'm* not enough for you without having to forsake every edict I've been given, then I will do the hardest thing I've ever done... and I will leave you, Ben."

The words stunned him much more than he expected them to. It wasn't like he hadn't considered the possibility. But to hear her actually say it...

Something snapped in him then. Or maybe it solidified. Like water finally freezing into solid ice. Eden was *his* angel. Sent for him and him alone, whether she realized it or not. Whatever it took, Benjamin was never going to let her go.

Wickedness has a way of sneaking up on you. No one just decides one day that they're going to turn bad. It happens a little at a time. Like an apple rotting on the ground.

For Benjamin Parker, it happened over the course of spring, summer, and fall in the year 1956. Little by little, his heart had turned frigid well before the first flake of snow dropped from the Maryland sky.

Eden had never budged on her refusal to do what he asked. It was near the end of summer when Benjamin gave up trying. He'd done just enough ever since then to delay her leaving, shown her just enough warmth to keep her hoping the fire might be rekindled. All the while, his mind was already made up.

The only problem that had held things up for so long was how he planned to do it. There was no way to force her. Eden would die before she did what he wanted. He knew that without having to make her prove it.

For months, it seemed there was no answer. In his desperation, Benjamin's anger had only grown. He would lie awake at night, seething and hating Eden's presence there beside him. He relished in daydreams of rolling over on top of her and choking the life from her just like she had choked the life from him. It was in those darkest hours that he began to hear the whispers.

They'd been almost imperceptible at first. Just a distant, airy hiss in the silence of the night. For a while, it had been maddening trying to discern what they said. But then a few words here and there started to come in clear.

Just his name at first, murmured from the shadows while he lay in bed. Then Eden's name, and a few more random, meaningless utterances. Last month, the whisperers had finally shown themselves.

They appeared to him like pillars of the blackest smoke in vaguely human form. Each night after Eden fell asleep, they would drop from the ceiling, rise from the floor, and slip through the walls to surround his bed. Six of them, all identical. All speaking with one voice. And the things they spoke now that Benjamin could see and hear them clearly awoke in him desires so dark it frightened him to know they existed.

The shadow beings—*demons;* he knew what they were—promised him the paradise he'd longed for ever since learning Eden was capable of delivering it. But not in the form he'd dreamt of. Not consciously at least. Theirs was a vision born from the blackest depths of his soul. A place where no desire would ever be denied to him. A world that existed solely for his pleasure.

They spoke, too, of what it would cost. What it would take to build this kingdom. Bending reality itself to his will would not come easy, they said. It would require a sacrifice of the highest value.

Except Benjamin wasn't even sure how much he truly valued her anymore. Not after all that his visitors had shown him, and the newly discovered desires those visions awakened. They had assured him it wouldn't matter, had told him that his hate for her would only make the process easier if he allowed it to fester. It mattered not how much the sacrifice cost him personally; there was still nothing they wouldn't give him in exchange for an angel's blood.

He didn't know exactly how he was going to do it yet. How he'd *be required* to do it. His visitors had not yet provided their full instructions. But he already knew by the nature they'd revealed that it would not be merciful. The sacrifice they required would be more than blood alone; pain would also have to be in the offering.

Watching her sleep soundly beside him in the dim, blue hue of moonlight through the bedroom window, Benjamin felt a stab of guilt. However badly she'd wronged him—and she *had* wronged him—she didn't deserve what was coming to her.

At this, the shadows gathered around his bed flared like flames in the wind. He could sense their outrage, an admonishment for his weakness. It didn't matter what one deserved, they told him, speaking directly to his soul. No one ever gets what they deserve. They get what they take.

And Benjamin was going to take it all.

"Show me the way," he whispered into the darkness. Beside him, Eden stirred and rolled into him in her sleep. But the feeling of her warmth against him did not waver his conviction. "I am ready."

By the way the room began to resonate with sinister energy, he could tell his visitors believed him. He had at last earned their trust.

Benjamin gasped as they entered him. A feeling like ice water shooting through his veins seized his muscles and sucked the wind from his lungs. He felt like screaming, but his mouth hung slack, his tongue limp and useless.

He passed out. In the moment, it seemed certain this was death.

When his awareness returned and he saw for the first time the warped and twisted faces of those shadows he had embraced—welcomed in—a torrent of regret swept through him.

They did not allow this feeling to persist. As the vision of what he must do—step by awful step—consumed him, Benjamin realized in some faraway corner of his mind that he no longer had a choice. He'd made his choice already, just seconds ago when his will was still his own. And now the time for turning back had passed.

It took Benjamin almost three days to build the structure he'd been told to create. He had followed the blueprint etched into his brain with painstaking meticulousness, refusing to let some error or technicality negate the contract. By the time the structure was complete, it looked exactly as it had in the vision they'd shown him.

Benjamin wiped his brow and took a step back, tilting his head to appraise it. The two beams he'd cemented to the ground stood exactly twelve feet tall. Between them was a pile of sticks about the size of a small wagon—exactly six hundred and sixty-six of them all fastened together with twine into miniature crosses. A ladder was propped against the pile and led up to a small platform, both of these also fashioned from dry wood.

There were four holes drilled all the way through the beams—two per beam with one near the top and one near the middle—and four ropes strung through them, each one ending in a tightly wound noose. The ropes were to be soaked in water just before the ritual commenced. It would end when the last one of them burned through.

Benjamin had built this fearsome structure right in the front yard, just as he'd been told. Had Eden seen it, she probably would have run and never looked back. But making sure that didn't happen had been step one, before the building ever started.

He looked at the barn and pictured her in there, chained to the plow. It would be time to bring her food and water soon. Not that it mattered with what the night held in store, but he intended to be as kind to her as possible. Right up until he no longer had a choice.

He took one last look at the structure—the altar on which she was to be offered—and felt a shudder pass through his bones. Then he hastily dusted off his clothes and went back inside.

He fixed a sandwich with ham from the smokehouse and a slice of ruby red tomato from the garden. It was pretty pitiful as far as last meals go, but Eden had always been the cook.

The walk to the barn was marked by dread and shame. He hated the way she looked at him, had avoided going near her as much as possible these past three days. It was clear he had already hurt her more than the coming flames ever could.

He stepped into the barn and saw her with her back against the plow blade. Eden looked up at him through strands of disheveled hair, but Benjamin dropped his eyes to the ground.

He set the plate with the sandwich on it and a cup of water on the dirt beside her. She didn't seem to care. Benjamin turned away, unable to bear her gaze any longer.

"Talk to me," she said as he started to leave the barn. Her voice was hoarse. Weak and defeated. "Please, Ben. Don't I deserve that?"

Benjamin sighed and rubbed his weary eyes. They'd done this already, more than once, and it wasn't going to change anything this time around either. He almost just kept walking. But like all the times before, guilt made him turn back around.

"What is there to talk about? It's too late. Even if I wanted to..."

"But you don't. Do you?"

"Don't what, Eden?"

"Want to."

Benjamin gnawed at the corner of his dry bottom lip, peeling back a layer of chapped skin between his teeth. There was nothing else to say.

"They are lying to you, Ben."

These words, the terrible confidence with which she spoke them, made his blood run cold. He'd considered the possibility—considered it constantly these past three nights while he lay awake listening to their whispers—and it was his greatest fear.

"No, I…I won't believe it."

Eden leaned forward, her pleading eyes still fixed on him. The chain around her ankle rustled and clinked until she had stretched it as far as it would allow. "Everything they promised you, it's all a lie. Listen to me. I am begging you. Whatever comes from what they've told you to do, it will not be what they showed you. They don't have the authority, Ben! And nothing good could ever come from something so evil."

"No." Benjamin said it emphatically this time. He wouldn't hear it, wouldn't even entertain the idea. Not now, when the time for turning back had already passed.

"It's not too late," Eden said. For not the first time in their relationship, Benjamin wondered if she could read his thoughts. "They've told you it is, but that's a lie, too. You can change your mind."

Benjamin didn't believe this either. Not when he could still feel them watching him. Could feel the weight of their determination pressing against his soul like the pressure of the ocean's deepest, darkest depths. The thought of resisting—kicking up and swimming toward the light he could no longer see—was almost laughable.

"Tonight..." he started. He could hardly bring himself to say it. Not directly anyway. "Tonight is when it happens."

Eden said nothing. She wouldn't resist, Benjamin knew. Not even when the time came to fasten her to the pyre. And for this, he was glad; he didn't know if his heart could take the pain.

"I love you, Ben," she finally said. "Even now."

The words hit him hard. Caught him completely unexpecting. By reflex, he almost said it back. He'd always said it back before. But this time he just stood there, breathing heavily. Finally, he turned his back to her and left.

There were no stars in the sky tonight. No sliver of a moon. This was the first thing Benjamin had noticed as he stepped out into the cool night air. Darkness swallowed him the moment he opened the door, and he soaked in it, not turning on the flashlight in his hand just yet. Without seeing where he was going, he followed the path he knew by heart from the house to the barn where Eden was chained.

She did not resist as he unlocked her shackles and led her to the base of the pyre outside the barn. Not physically. Not verbally. In fact, she never spoke a word. She just stared straight ahead at the structure alight in the flashlight's beam. When they reached it, Benjamin saw her lift her eyes to the sky and hold them there for a long moment's time.

"I'm..." Benjamin started. *Sorry* was the rest. But what a useless thing to say. Eden had it right; there was nothing left for either of them to say.

He took her hand, and she let him. He placed it in the loop of rope hanging from the structure's left beam, then tightened the noose around her wrist.

He didn't have to grab her other hand. She reached it out for him to take. Another gut punch of shame nearly sent him to his knees. He almost wished she'd fight back. At least curse his name and the day she met him. Give him one small reason—any reason—to become angry so he could cling to the feeling long enough to see this through.

Instead, she never even flinched as he fastened her feet to the second set of ropes. He might have mistaken her demeanor for calm acceptance—peace, perhaps—if it weren't for the way her heart visibly pounded beneath the bodice of her soiled dress.

When he pulled the ropes and stretched her into an X-shaped contortion, he was careful not to stretch them too tight. Because...

Because he didn't want to hurt her. It hit him then how meaningless this was in the shadow of what came next. That moment was the closest he came to turning back.

But then, from the corner of his eye, Benjamin saw them. Or sensed them, more like. They melded perfectly into the darkness, but he could feel them all around him, watching. A chill spread through the air. It turned the night breeze frigid and prickled his skin as if their arrival had dropped the temperature ten or twenty degrees.

Benjamin kept his eyes on his feet, fearful to look at them. Fearful of the darkness where they hid and the darkness he felt spreading from them. He half-ran, half-stumbled to the bucket of water he'd set near the pyre. What he wanted more than anything right now was for this terrible thing to be over. He wondered how long it would last—how long *she* would last—and prayed to the very God he'd forsaken that she would succumb quickly.

His hands shook as he splashed the water onto the ropes, and he almost dropped the pail. There was barely enough light from the flashlight he'd set on the ground to see what he was doing. Though he missed a few times, he managed to soak all four ropes.

The water dripping from them and a stir of wind were the night's only sounds. Eden's eyes were closed now. Her lips moved gently but formed no words. Benjamin knew who she was speaking to. He almost expected a bolt of lightning to strike down from the sky and fry him where he stood. He almost wished it would. But none came.

Benjamin picked up the flashlight and shined it on a steel jerry can next to the pyre, freshly filled just this morning with gasoline from Paul Smith's station down the road. It seemed like such a horrible thing now, this ordinary object he'd owned ever since he bought the farm. It made him nauseous to look at it, and when he picked it up, it felt much heavier than it had earlier.

"It'll be over soon," he said, though he hadn't meant to say it aloud. He repeated it again and again in his head as he worked his way around the pyre, dousing the platform and ladder and branches with fuel.

From the shadows all around, his visitors watched and waited. Benjamin could sense their anticipation, thrumming in the air. What came next wasn't the final step in the process they'd shown him, but it was the true point of no return.

He reached into his pocket and pulled out a Zippo lighter. The same one he'd used to light the occasional cigar, and Eden the occasional candle. He opened its cap and flicked the flint. The spark caught. A ribbon of flame danced from the end of the cotton wick.

In the dim glow of it, he could see her watching him. He waited for her to say something. To try one last time to talk him out of it, or maybe twist the knife in his soul again like she had in the barn when she told him she loved him. But her final words were spoken already, and they had not been meant for him. Unable to bear it any longer, Benjamin looked away.

Voices from the darkness urged him on. They practically screamed in his ears. The paradise they'd promised him seemed so far away. No longer worth the cost now that the time to pay it had come.

But Benjamin was too afraid to deny them.

"God forgive me."

A flick of his wrist sent the Zippo sailing through the air. It landed at the base of the pyre, flame still flickering. A heartbeat later, a whoosh of fire lit up his eyes. Benjamin fell to the hard, dry soil and wailed like a child as he watched her burn.

She never screamed. If she had, he might not have survived it. It seemed like such a thing would break his heart in a literal, lethal sense. Yet it took so horribly long for the flames to finally take her. Benjamin begged for time to pass faster, for it to end, but the longest seconds of his life turned into minutes before it was over.

It took even longer for the ropes binding her upright to burn through and her charred body to fall into the still-flaming heap. Benjamin knew what he was expected to do next. But the fire still burned so hot he had to shield his face with his arm as he approached it. He stopped a few feet from the edge of the pyre and turned his head away, choking on the smoke. Choking back sobs.

Continue, spoke a voice—spoke six different voices—in his head. Benjamin feared what they would do if he didn't obey more than he feared the flames.

Burning timbers snapped beneath his boots as he scrambled up the pyre, nearly tripping him. The heat singed every inch of his uncovered skin, and even his thick clothing couldn't block it all the way. Eden's foot dangled over the edge of the pyre. Benjamin reached for it, but the hot, blackened skin peeled off in his hands.

His clothes were starting to catch fire. His face and hands were already reddening. Benjamin gritted through the pain and wrapped his hands around her leg again, with a much firmer grip this time. Then he pulled so hard he tumbled back off the pyre.

Benjamin rolled in the dirt at its base to extinguish his flaming clothes. He whimpered and coughed and forced himself back to his feet before those wretched voices could tell him to.

Getting Eden's corpse all the way to the well was a miserable exercise. Her flesh was so hot he couldn't bear to hold onto her for long. Her body kept coming apart each time he tried to drag or lift it—like meat from the oven so well-cooked it was falling off the bone. When he finally got her to the well and lifted her up over the edge, Benjamin didn't hesitate a blink before pushing her over. He didn't want to have to look at what he'd done to her a moment longer.

When he heard the splash, he knew that it was over. He'd done everything his dark visitors had asked of him. Followed their instructions to the letter. But the relief he'd expected never came. Instead, Benjamin fell to his knees and broke down into another bout of wracking sobs.

Darkness pressed in on him. The shadows that had watched him carry out their demands advanced until they encircled him, blocking out the light from the fire. They swirled around him in a whirlwind that continued to pick up speed. He could feel the wind of it against his blistered skin and could hear its whine growing louder.

All the oxygen left the air and joined the vortex, leaving Benjamin gasping for breath. Explosions like artillery fire detonated in his head, then the grating scream of metal grinding against metal.

When the whirlwind dissipated and Benjamin at last gathered the courage to open his eyes, it looked as though nothing had changed. The embers from the pyre still glowed and flickered. The sky was still just as shrouded and dark as before. No glowing rays of heavenly light. No roaring flames of hellfire either.

Yet something *had* changed. Something monumental. Benjamin could feel it in every nerve. He could almost taste it in the air. This was not the home he knew anymore. Every stone and grain of dust, though still in the same place as before, seemed altered in some indescribable way.

Poisoned was the word that came to mind, and dread unlike anything he had ever felt settled in his bowels. He couldn't stand to admit it yet, clung desperately to fading flickers of hope, but his thoughts went there anyway: Eden had been right.

They had tricked him, just like she said they would. Those whispering shadows who had promised pleasures beyond comprehension were now nowhere to be seen.

"I tried to warn you, Ben," spoke a voice much different than theirs. One that brought a stream of fresh tears from his eyes. "I tried to tell you that only evil can come from evil."

If he strained his eyes, he could see her there standing in front of him. An outline glowing faintly in the darkness. Like starlight molded into her form.

Benjamin lifted a trembling hand to touch her, but his fingers met no resistance. The pale light just danced across his skin without any sensation. He could feel her in a different way, though. One much more profound that made him look away.

"Listen to me," he heard her speak. Sorrow colored every word, yet the power on that voice was enough for Benjamin to feel it all the way down in his bones. The light shining on him began to blaze much brighter, too. And when Benjamin lifted his eyes again, shielding them against its glare, he saw a form much different than that of the woman he'd once loved. One incomprehensible: a wholly unfathomable geometry of fiery wheels and hypnotic eyes.

"Benjamin William Parker," bellowed the angel of God. "There is now a choice for you to make."

CHAPTER TWENTY-ONE

Jason sat down on a fallen tree outside the entrance to Damien Winters' bunker and watched the darkness turn to daylight in a blink. This was the first time he'd survived to see the end of The Flip. The first time it had ended in any other way than his death and subsequent resurrection sometime later once it was over.

He paused there for a while and took it in. Collected himself, as much as he was able. Then he stood and began his journey out of the forest.

He knew exactly where he needed to go. So much knowledge had returned to him it was overwhelming. As the leaves and branches crunched beneath his steady footsteps, Jason tried to let his mind go blank. The wind and forest sounds and the smell of earthy soil were all he tried to focus on. Yet with every step closer he drew to his destination, the rest became harder to ignore.

Memories he had buried beneath fathoms of crushing darkness were rising like bubbles from the deep. An entire history—*his* history—coming back to remind him why he'd worked so hard to forget it. Jason gritted his teeth. Tears wet his eyes, and it was all he could do to keep walking when his knees felt a calling for the ground.

Eventually, the forest broke. He could see a grassy field stretching out before him. On the other side of it, hardly more than a dot on the horizon, were the skeletal remains of a house burned to its foundation. Somewhere amidst that rubble, Old Man Benjamin likely still sat. But Jason wasn't coming back for him. There was someone else he needed to see. A reunion a lifetime in the making. One he dreaded immensely in light of all the ways he'd failed.

It felt like crossing the field took an eternity. By the time he reached the crumbling remnants of Benjamin's house, Jason was crumbling himself. He staggered across the dirt and ash, weeping as he walked.

He saw Benjamin from the corner of his eye. He heard him say something that never registered. The old man approached him, but Jason kept on walking. He was almost to the well. The circle of stones that formed its mouth glistened in the sunlight.

Jason set his hands against them and peered down into the dark cavity. He could feel her down there. Whatever Damien Winters had injected him with, it had heightened his senses for such things. Brought back more than memories, but abilities he'd lost along with them.

"Son!" At last, the volume of Benjamin's voice was enough to penetrate Jason's thoughts. "Listen to me, damn it!"

Jason gripped the well stones harder beneath his calloused hands, making sure his fingers found purchase. In his current state, it would take a little effort to vault himself over the edge.

"Don't do it!" Benjamin pleaded. "God, I can't take another one of those things here!"

Jason didn't know what he was talking about. Or maybe he did. He'd learned a lot, after all. And he would soon find out the rest.

Just as he felt the old man's hand touch his arm, Jason pulled away and hoisted himself up onto the edge of the well. He sat there for a moment, long enough to draw a deep breath and observe the look of horror on Benjamin's face. Then he slid off the edge and into the mouth of the well.

He closed his eyes as the water below rushed up to greet him: a fallen angel, falling once again.

CHAPTER TWENTY-TWO

There was no splash. No splatter either. One moment he was falling, the next moment he wasn't. Floating was what it felt like now. Floating in a pool of liquid light. He could feel it warming every inch of his skin, and when he opened his eyes, its golden glow was all that he could see.

A sound reverberated through the otherworldly medium. Something like horns and voices and thunder all mingled together. Distorted and deafeningly loud. So loud he could feel it in his skull, and every hair on his body stood rigid.

From within the swirling waters of light, a being emerged. One formed of shining eyes and turning wheels assembled together into a shape that strained the mind to look at. And yet he recognized this being. At one time, he had known her as a friend.

Shame washed over him in crippling waves. It had been so long since he'd felt such a thing—so long since he'd felt *anything* but the searing hate he'd tempered himself in—that he couldn't help but cry out.

His cries echoed through the waters of light and turned into ripples. The ripples turned into waves, and soon it felt like all the light was draining away. Rushing out as if someone had pulled the drain at the bottom of this strange reality. When all of it was gone, he still remained—no longer floating but standing now. Standing in a garden that sprouted fruits and flowers of all varieties for as far as he could see. A woman stood in front of him. One with ivory skin and flaming hair and emerald eyes. Even in this human form, he still recognized her.

"Hello, Ezekiel," the woman said. "I've been waiting for you."

That wasn't his name. Not anymore. But it used to be. A long, dark lifetime ago. Hearing it again, the waves of shame returned.

"Do you remember me?"

He did. He remembered everything. Much of it—all that came before this mortal existence—was impossible to comprehend, even though the memories were clear. He felt like an insect suddenly recalling that it used to be a human and trying to understand with a mind never designed for the task all the things that other life entailed.

"What...what should I call you?" he asked the woman. He knew her name, but it was not a sound anything this side of Heaven could form.

"You can call me Eden. Now, what should I call you? Ezekiel Hartman...or Jason Baker?"

"I am not that man!" He practically wept the words.

"You didn't use to be." So much disappointment came through in her tone he could hardly take it. "When you lost your way, you took that name. Borrowed it from someone you looked up to. But it was still you. The things you did as Jason Baker were still *your* actions."

He covered his eyes with his hands and pulled at the bangs of his hair, shaking his head not in denial but in disbelief at all that he had done. "It was too much! I couldn't...couldn't take it. I wasn't ready for it all!"

"I know, my dear friend." Her eyes betrayed her sorrow. Even the warm wind that moved through the leaves of the garden seemed to carry sorrow on its current. "I know what you endured."

He didn't want to remember it, but it came back anyway. All those buried memories of his time at the orphanage. His time with Oliver Lench and the bullies who used to mock him and the foster parents who used to whip him and scold him and never show him anything close to love. It was too much. Too much then and too much now. How could he have been expected to do anything but drown that pain with whatever worked to numb it?

"It is a dangerous thing when an angel sent to earth abandons their mission," Eden said. "Without that tether to hold us, there is no limit to how far we will fall."

His mission. Up until now, he'd kept his strength, but when he thought of that purpose he'd abandoned, he could stay standing no longer. Trembling, he lowered himself to his knees and buried his face in the soft, sweet-smelling grass at Eden's feet.

"It should have been you that stopped that bus," she said. "When you fell, another, who took the name Amanda Williams, was sent in your place. But somewhere in your soul you still felt a calling to be on that road at that time. And you intercepted her. When all those children needed a guardian angel, it was a demon that arrived instead."

"I'm so sorry." He meant it now that it was possible to feel such things again. Now that all the blood-and-drug-and-liquor-soaked walls he'd built were crumbling.

"I know you are. But know, too, that there can be no repentance without atonement."

"Have I not suffered enough?" He didn't intend it as a challenge. More like a plea for mercy.

There was sorrow in her eyes still, but a steadfastness, too, that chilled his heart. "You have endured an entire lifetime of suffering, my dear friend. But only *one lifetime*. How many lives of others did you ruin in that span?"

"I don't know," he said, shaking his head against the grassy ground. "I don't know."

"The answer is four hundred and eleven. Only seven were killed by your own hand, but there are exactly four hundred and eleven lives you destroyed as a result of those actions. And that is the most merciful accounting Heaven can offer you, my friend. It is hard to even begin unraveling the web of pain you've woven. All the countless lives that have been impacted because of the seven you snuffed out."

It felt wrong to discuss these terrible things in a beautiful place like this, like the breeze that carried on it such sweet flower scents and birdsong couldn't possibly be the same one carrying these damning words. It made hearing them feel all the more shameful.

"What will happen to me?" He knew what he deserved, the pit of darkness where all fallen angels are bound, and he dreaded her answer. But this sentence to Hell that he expected was not what came.

"You are going to be given a choice," Eden said. "It is the same choice offered to Benjamin, and Samuel, and Oliver, and all the others you met in that terrible place. If any of you are to ever leave it, one of you must be willing to make atonement."

"What kind of atonement?" Jason liked to think there could be no alternative worse than going back to that farm, but the sinking feeling in his chest suggested otherwise.

"Only what justice demands. No less and no more. There were four hundred and eleven lives that you ruined. If you are going to atone for that and earn the release of yourself and the others, you must be willing to walk in all of their shoes. Willing to live out those lifetimes, one after the other, and experience for yourself all the destruction you have wrought."

"*No*." He wept into the grass. He couldn't do it. Just one lifetime in human flesh had broken him beyond comprehension. To suffer four hundred and eleven of them...the farm and all its torments paled in comparison. For an angel like him, Hell itself paled in comparison. "Why has no one else taken this offer?" But he already knew the simple answer: none of them had been willing either.

"Some owe debts much greater than yours," Eden answered. "Yet some were willing at first. Until they learned of the alternative."

"What alternative?" It felt shameful asking, but he had to know.

Eden took her time answering. Whatever the alternative was, he could tell it burdened her to offer it.

"There are wicked beings that tricked a man I once loved into creating that place you are all trapped within. The place I am now responsible for overseeing until the day it is undone. These beings offer their own way out. If you choose to take their bargain, they will remake you in their image. You will become a monster each time the event you know as The Flip takes place, just like those whose hands you've been suffering beneath. And you will spend the rest of your days trying to make life on that farm as miserable as possible for all the rest in the fleeting hope that eventually someone other than you will choose the harder path."

The Slaver and The Scarecrow, The Priestess and The Scientist and The Ice Cream Man—all their hideous faces flashed across his mind. He'd thought they were mad, or maybe just evil by design. But that wasn't it. All of them were locked in a gruesome game of chicken, tormenting him and the old man and each other and whoever else arrived on that farm to try and make them break.

"What about Benjamin?" He had never turned into one of those things, and yet he was still trapped there. "Which offer did he choose?"

The sorrow in Eden's eyes deepened immeasurably when he mentioned the old man's name. Was he the one she'd been talking about? The man she had once loved.

"Neither. Benjamin believes if he endures to the end that I will have mercy on him. He doesn't realize that there is no end. Or that mercy without true repentance is not mine to give."

"You tried, though. You tried one time to stop it." When Jason—a person the man kneeling in the grass now hardly identified with anymore—had jammed that probe into The Scientist's skull, he'd seen what happened to Aiko. The mission she'd been sent to accomplish.

"We tried so many more times than once, my dear friend," Eden said. "You were all given *so many* chances to change your path before it led to that farm. And if just one of you, *just one*, had not done what you did, it would have changed everything. All your lives are connected. You all have each other to blame just as much as yourselves."

"I don't understand." It was clear to him the role that Oliver Lench had played in sending him down the road to Hell, but he could see no connection between the rest.

"If Benjamin Parker had not prevented me from completing my mission, your parents would have never died of cancer, and you would have never stepped foot in that orphanage. Another named Farrah Gosling was sent to save you. To befriend you and help you find your way again, back when there was still hope. She was shot as a teenager by Leon Kingsley before your paths could cross.

"You already know about Aiko Fujimoto, how she was sent as an emissary to that farm, and how Damien Winters stopped her. What you don't know is that if you had completed your mission,

Dr. Winters would never have been born. A young woman in Miami would have married a boy that died on that school bus instead of marrying Damien's grandfather.

"I could go on, but I think you see the picture. That's the beauty of good and the scourge of evil, my dear friend: a single act of either can ripple across space and time so much farther than one ever anticipates."

The weight of it all bore on him so heavily he felt pinned to the ground. If staying there forever with his face in the soil, pleading forgiveness for the rest of time, had been one of the options before him, that's the one he would have taken. But it was not. And when a gust of wind colder than any before it moved through the grass, it seemed somehow a sign that his time here was drawing to a close.

"I am sorry," Eden said. "I wish humanity had treated you kinder. I wish you had treated them kinder even so. But now it is time for you to choose."

CHAPTER TWENTY-THREE

Sitting in the dirt and ash where his home once stood, Benjamin watched and waited. His eyes were fixed on the well from which all his sorrows sprung. He tried not to get his hopes up; five times already he had felt such hope only to watch nightmare after nightmare climb out of that well.

He wondered what Jason's number would be—the number of lives he'd ruined. The number of lifetimes lived he would owe. Whatever it was, it couldn't possibly be greater than Benjamin's number.

He had lied before, lashed out in moments of weakness like all imperfect people do, but murdering Eden had been his only mortal sin. Yet had anyone in all of history ever committed a sin so consequential? Eden Donnovan would have wiped away one of the world's greatest evils over a century before humanity figured it out on their own. Exactly five hundred and fifteen million, six thousand and seventy-three lives would have been saved. Benjamin knew that number as well as his own birth date and name.

Five hundred and fifteen million, six thousand and seventy-three was *his* number.

Thinking about it made his head spin. How could a person even come to grips with such a thing? All the pain he'd caused, all the pain he'd have to live through if he accepted Eden's offer—it was impossible to comprehend. Like trying to grasp how large the ocean is, or how far away the stars.

He took a long, deep breath that turned into a quivering moan when he let it out. The air was cold. Colder, it seemed, than it had been just a minute ago. He looked up at the sky, but the sun was still there, shining gold behind thin clouds.

Would it stay that way much longer? Benjamin didn't think it would. Soon, all of reality would flip on its axis like a carcass on a spit. The sun would darken, and the stars that replaced it would all shine blood red. Then whatever abomination those dark spirits molded from Jason's form would climb out of the well and come for him.

The more time that passed, the more sure of it Benjamin became. It was happening already. He could sense it in the air. Somewhere—at the bottom of the well was how to get there, but the place itself existed far away—Jason's transformation had begun. He might have had no way of knowing this for certain, but Benjamin was certain anyway.

So when a sinking feeling like falling from a cliff pulled at his organs, Benjamin felt no disappointment or surprise. From the moment Jason went down that well, he'd never expected anything else. Who would choose a burden as heavy as what Eden required when tormenting others until someone else chose it instead was an offer on the table? If there existed a person who would, they were the kind of person who would've never ended up on this farm in the first place.

Darkness settled over the land in falling curtains. The air turned frigid and foul. So cold that even the hot tears spilling down his cheeks began to freeze before they could fall, and his heaving breaths came out white smoke.

From the well, a blue-green light began to shine. Shadows flickered from within it as something down there started to move. Benjamin heard grunts and the scrape of boots and fingernails against the stones.

He could have run. He probably could've even gotten away for a while. He was tired of running and hiding, though. All it did was prolong the inevitable. This time, he was going to sit there on the ground and let the inevitable come.

A hand appeared over the edge of the well, dripping wet and glistening in the ghostly light, then another beside it. Benjamin saw purple veins bulging from speckled, gray skin and cable-like tendons tensing as the thing hoisted itself up over the edge.

Its head looked only half-human—a vague semblance of Jason's features but discolored and disfigured and everything twice the size as before. A long, bumpy tongue parted its blue lips and slipped across teeth that had been filed to triangle points. Eyes the color of bloody egg yolks slowly scanned the world outside the well. Then they locked on Benjamin.

Blades jingled as the monster started forward. All manner of them hung from loops on the long, black apron it wore—cleavers and skinning knives, meat hooks and bone saws. They gleamed in the sickly moonlight, their edges as of yet unstained.

The Butcher. That's what this one was called. Benjamin had never chosen any of their names. At least that's not what it felt like. It felt like the names just came to him the moment they climbed out of the well, chosen not by him but by the spirits that birthed these monsters. And the name those spirits had chosen for their newest child seemed fitting in every way.

The Butcher shook his head like a wet dog as he approached, sending beads of well water soaring from the matted cords of his long, dark hair. Something else shook loose, too. A pair of protrusions on his back that Benjamin hadn't noticed before. They looked like folded-up wings. Pitch black like raven wings. Or the wings of a death angel.

When the monster's shadow fell over where he sat, Benjamin lifted his eyes, trailing them up the thing's apron and all the chilling instruments that dangled from it until their eyes met.

"Hello, old man."

"Hello, son."

The Butcher grabbed hold of him, wrapping his cold, wet fingers tight around Benjamin's arm. Benjamin didn't resist. He just staggered to his feet when the monster lifted him and let it drag him away.

He knew where they were going, even if he didn't know what it would look like when they got there. It would be another terrible pocket of this place, created at the same moment The Butcher was born. Probably some dilapidated packing house with mold and bloodstains all over the walls and rusted hooks on chains hanging from the ceiling, if Benjamin had to guess.

But as they drew closer to the well the monster had just climbed from, he realized what was actually going on.

Benjamin's heart sank. "No...no, I won't do it!" he shouted as The Butcher hauled him to the edge of the well.

"*You will.*"

The hand around Benjamin's arm tightened, and The Butcher lifted him off the ground like a sack of groceries. His feet grazed the rough, stone surface of the well's rim, then they were dangling over the dark circle.

"Not this!" Benjamin pleaded. "I can't! I can't see her again!"

But he knew the words were pointless before they ever left his mouth. Benjamin felt the grip on his arm loosen, felt weightless for a split second before gravity took over, then felt himself begin to fall.

CHAPTER TWENTY-FOUR

Benjamin's breath hitched. It felt like he'd been plunged into icy water. Not an unreasonable thing to expect when you're tossed into a well, but the feeling wasn't literal.

What Benjamin expected to see when he opened his eyes was the garden where she'd met him the last time he'd had the strength to face her. Instead, he was sitting at his kitchen table. And she sat across from him.

She looked just like she did when he first met her. Not a blemish on her fair skin or a single strand of snow in her fiery hair. Even the kitchen looked like it once had, the wood of the table, cabinets, and floor all new and polished instead of scuffed and worn. A painfully familiar warmth filled the space again. One it had only ever known when Eden lived there.

"It's been a very long time, Ben."

"I...I know." It was hard to speak. So much emotion roiled inside of him, it crowded out the words.

"You've changed so much."

"You haven't changed at all."

"I have, though, Ben. I've probably changed even more than you."

Benjamin didn't want to believe it. She was perfect before she met him. If she had changed, then he was the one to blame.

"I shouldn't be here," he said. "It wasn't my...he threw me down here. Jason Baker. *The Butcher*."

"I know," Eden said. "He wasn't always a butcher, though. The world changed him, too. I'd hoped he would have the strength to find his way again, but he was too far gone."

"He's going to tear me apart, Eden. You know that. All of them...they're not ever going to stop. I...I can't take it anymore!"

Trying to guilt her was a sickening shame, but he couldn't help it. Now that he was thinking about The Butcher and all the other demons awaiting his return, dread had gripped his heart.

"You don't have to."

"No," Benjamin said, shaking his head. "Your way is no better."

"It is. I promise it is, Ben. You have to trust me."

"Five hundred and fifteen million, six thousand and seventy-three." Benjamin whispered the number with horrified reverence.

"Yes. And you must be willing to bear every one of their burdens. If you are, then you will find peace."

"It's unthinkable."

"It is what true repentance requires."

Benjamin realized he was trying not to cry in front of her. As if time really had been rolled back and he was a young man again, not wanting to look weak in front of his new bride. When he realized how foolish this was, the tears began to fall.

"I made one mistake, Eden! I did one terrible, unforgivable thing. But how could I have known that this would be the cost?"

She looked sorrowful, regretful on his behalf, but—like all the times before he'd made such pleas—unpersuaded. "You knew what I was. What I was sent for. You understood what it would cost the world. You just didn't realize what it would cost *you*."

Benjamin wept harder. Every word burned like arrows in his heart.

"And it isn't just the world you sinned against that night, Ben. You murdered a holy servant of God. You couldn't possibly understand the weight of that transgression. When angels bleed, all of Heaven trembles."

Benjamin was the one trembling now, though. This is why he would have rather that monster carved him apart with every blade on its apron than make him come here.

"But do you know what's the most heartbreaking part of all?" Eden continued anyway. "It's that you could have had the paradise you longed for, Ben. I don't just mean the one you and I could have created here together, difficult though it would have been. I mean the whole world. If it wasn't for the same greed and cold-heartedness that drove you to do what you did, the whole world could be a paradise."

"If I could take it back, you know I would." Taking it back was all he'd ever dreamed of.

"I know you would," Eden said. "But everyone feels that way when their day of judgment comes. And there is no taking back what's been done."

"What's the point then, Eden?" Benjamin almost choked on the words. "If I do what you're asking me to, what will change?"

"You will. If you are willing to bear in full the pain you forced on others, then *you* will have changed."

She wanted so badly for him to accept it. Even with his eyes blurred by tears and his pulse ringing in his ears, Benjamin could tell. After what he'd done to her, it tore him to know how much she still cared.

"I loved you," he said. No matter what happened next, he needed her to know. "It was real. I…I ruined it. I let it die. But it was real."

"It was real, Ben."

A fresh wave of sobs spilled out as his heart tore open even wider. What he wouldn't give for time to be rolled back. If a chance to start life over with her was what she offered, no price would've been too high.

But even if her forgiveness was the only thing to gain, maybe it was still worth the cost. That might not be the reason she wanted him to have, but wasn't it the same? Wasn't love the reason either way?

"I am…" His heart sank when he thought of all the sorrow he'd endure, all the death and pain, so he focused on her instead. "I am willing to atone for what I've done."

"*Ben,*" she said. He noticed that his eyes were no longer the only ones teary. The way she looked at him, the way she spoke his name, bled with pent-up emotion. "That is all that was ever required."

Benjamin wasn't sure what she meant at first. And he didn't get the chance to ask.

In a blink, she was gone. He never saw her vanish, even though he'd been looking at her the whole time. He just realized suddenly that he was sitting at the table alone. The rest—what she meant, what she'd meant all along—dawned on him a little at a time.

He stayed there for a while. Maybe it was only his imagination, but the warmth of her—her honey scent and the echo of her voice—seemed to linger for a time. When even these were gone and there were no more tears left for him to cry, Benjamin stood from the table and walked out the door.

The sun was shining when he stepped outside. Shining in a way it had not shined on this farm in decades. Trills and whistles, warbles and chirps, sounded from the woods around his home. It'd been so long since he heard it, it took him a moment to recognize the chorus as birdsong.

Other than the sunlight, the well was the first thing that caught his eye. Not because that's where Eden was anymore, he knew in his heart that she had left for good, but because of the items he noticed sitting on its rim.

Benjamin walked over and picked one of them up—a Bowie knife with the initials J.B. carved into its handle. The totems of all the others were lined up next to it: Samuel's whip, Hagar's amulet, Leon's hat, Damien's probe, and the keys to Oliver's truck. He could tell in the same way he sensed that Eden was gone that all of them were gone as well.

He didn't know what had happened to them any more than he knew what to expect when his own death came. If judgment still awaited any of them, he liked to think they'd at least get credit for time served.

Benjamin set the knife back down and lifted his eyes to look down the road that cut across his farm. It no longer seemed to stretch on forever. At its end, he could see a paved highway that had never been there before. A strange-looking car drove by, then disappeared into the distance. Benjamin felt a flash of fear when he thought about all the unknown that waited for him at the end of that road. Like Eden had said, there could be no undoing what had been done. His youth was gone, and the world had surely changed immeasurably in the time he'd been trapped here.

Then again, the world never really changed that much. Until people changed, it never would.

There weren't a lot of years left for him. So many he had lost. But however many remained, he was determined to spend every second on things that would make her proud.

"Goodbye, Eden," Benjamin whispered into the wind. Then he started walking down the road.

The End

ALSO BY
JOHN ASHLEY

NOVELS

The Dark Thing

A Nest of Broken Bones

SHORT STORIES AND NOVELLAS:

Deadbolt

The Girl in the Attic

JOHN ASHLEY is a freelance writer and indie author who lives in Springfield, Missouri. What started as a love for ghost stories and Goosebumps books turned into a lifelong passion for all things horror, and writing horror books is the bloody, beating heart of that passion. When he's not writing, John enjoys watching sports, spending time outdoors, and hanging out with his wife and their three pets.

For updates on new releases and other important news, join John Ashley's newsletter at johnashleyauthor.com.

Printed in Dunstable, United Kingdom

81567135R00160